# THE TUDOR GARDEN MYSTERY

When one of Sir Richard Alperton's house guests is murdered in the Tudor Garden at Grandchester Manor, police suspicion falls upon his son Robert. In desperation, Sir Richard turns to his friends Felix Heron and his wife Thelma to help clear his son's name. To the initial annoyance of the police, the private investigator and his wife join the house guests and set to work to solve the mystery. But when two more murders rapidly follow, it looks like the detective duo may finally have met their match . . .

GERALD VERNER

# THE TUDOR GARDEN MYSTERY

*Complete and Unabridged*

**LINFORD**
*Leicester*

First published in Great Britain

First Linford Edition
published 2015

A catalogue record for this book is available
from the British Library.

ISBN 978–1–4448–2593–0

Published by
F. A. Thorpe (Publishing)
Anstey, Leicestershire

Set by Words & Graphics Ltd.
Anstey, Leicestershire
Printed and bound in Great Britain by
T. J. International Ltd., Padstow, Cornwall

This book is printed on acid-free paper

# 1

It was one of those mornings in early spring when this uneasy and battered old world still seems a very pleasant place to live. In the country, and such open spaces as the destructive march of progress has not already destroyed, the swollen buds were bursting stickily into leaf, and the golden trumpets of the daffodils glowed in parks and small gardens, as though the sun had spilled lakes of yellow fire.

Felix Heron, looking out from the window of his flat across the park, and idly watching the passing traffic in Park Lane below, felt strongly disinclined to tackle the work that awaited him on his littered desk. It was mostly dull and uninteresting, and the lure of the morning was insistent.

Exactly what Felix Heron's business was caused a great deal of speculation among a great number of people. He was not an ordinary private investigator, he was not a solicitor, he was not a special agent, he was not in any way connected with the official police. Yet he combined nearly all these things in his daily work. In anything that was out of the ordinary in the way of crime, that the official police force found difficult to handle, or that the Foreign Office required delicately handled, he was consulted — rather in the manner of a medical specialist. Sometimes, he handled these assignments without leaving his pleasant flat; sometimes, he had to travel far afield. In all these activities he was assisted by his young and very beautiful wife, Thelma, and an able secretary named Harry. If this efficient person had any other name besides Harry it was never mentioned, either by himself or his employer.

He was an ugly man of approaching middle age, with strongly marked eyebrows and practically no hair on his head. His hands were large and clumsy-looking, but he could type accurately at great speed. Felix Heron delegated most of his routine work to Harry, but there was a certain amount of special and confidential letters and documents that he was forced to deal with himself.

With a sigh, he turned reluctantly away from the window and went over to the large carved-oak writing table that occupied the centre of the pleasant, book-lined room, and was about to seat himself in the padded leather chair when Harry came in quickly. He moved silently and with surprising swiftness for such a thick-set man.

'Just come,' he said briefly, putting a telegram down on the table in front of Heron. 'Any answer?'

Heron tore open the envelope and scanned the contents. 'No,' he said, 'there's no answer. Is Mrs. Heron in?'

'I'll see.' Harry was at the door and outside almost before he had finished speaking. Heron took a cigarette from the silver box on the writing table and lit it.

'You wanted me?' Thelma came over to his side. Without being tall, she gave the impression of litheness. Her dark hair held lights in it that suggested copper, and her very deep blue eyes were intelligent.

'Yes — look at that, dear.' He held out the wire.

She looked at it. 'From Alperton.' She looked up. 'He seems to be in trouble.'

Heron nodded. Sir Richard Alperton was a friend to both of them. He was the owner of a lovely old Tudor mansion in Oxfordshire, a beautiful period building which he had recently bought. Felix and his wife had spent a pleasant weekend there soon after he had acquired the place.

'Are you going?' she asked. 'It sounds urgent.'

'Yes. Alperton's not the type to ask for help over nothing.' He frowned and looked across at the window. 'It would be rather nice at Grandchester Manor just now, don't you think?'

A hint of laughter lit up her eyes. 'Any excuse to get away from London, eh?' she said.

'Wouldn't you like to go?'

'You know I would.'

'Very well, we'll go!' he said. 'But we'll try and find out a little more about this.' He flipped over the leaves of a telephone number index on the table. 'We'll ring up

4

and see what Alperton has to say.'

He found the number and lifted the receiver of the telephone. After several minutes, he looked up at his wife. 'Very strange,' he murmured.

'Can't you get through?

'The line is apparently out of order,' he answered, putting the receiver down.

'Out of order?' She raised her delicate eyebrows.

'Queer, isn't it?' He got up. 'How long will it be before you can be ready?'

'Fifteen minutes,' she answered promptly.

'Tell Harry to get the car round,' he said. 'Ask him to send a wire to Alperton saying we are on our way.'

Thelma nodded and went out. Heron stood for a moment rubbing his chin. Alperton was not the kind to panic over nothing, and there had been more than a hint of panic in the wording of that wire. He unlocked a drawer in the writing table. From it he took out a small, but very deadly, automatic and slipped it into his pocket.

It seemed unlikely that he would need

such a weapon — but it was as well to be prepared.

Later, he was glad that he had the weapon with him.

★ ★ ★

The powerful car sped along through the spring sunshine. Felix Heron was a fast driver but he never took foolish risks. He knew to a fraction just what the car was capable of and he kept well within the limit. Speed in itself is not dangerous, so long as it remains under complete control.

It was midday when they reached the outskirts of Grandchester. 'Not bad going,' said Heron, as they ran easily up the narrow High Street.

Thelma laughed. 'I know — you're a marvellous driver,' she said.

Heron grunted.

'Isn't that what you wanted me to say?' she inquired.

'There's no need to state the obvious,' he retorted.

From the village to the manor was

nearly a mile and a half. They turned into a narrow road that would bring them to the drive gates. It was little more than a lane, hedge-lined, and with scarcely enough room for two cars to pass. It led only to the elm avenue that twisted from the entrance gates to the house. They came in sight of these gates in a few minutes, wrought-iron and set between square pillars of mellow brick.

'Hello!' murmured Heron. 'It looks as if something pretty serious has happened.'

Thelma saw the uniformed constable standing near the lodge just inside, and nodded. The gates were open and the man stared hard at them as they drove past, but he made no effort to stop them.

The long drive bordered by ancient elms, just beginning to assume a mantle of green, stretched before them, and in a little while they came in sight of the house.

Grandchester Manor is noted among the architectural glories of England. It is pure Tudor, with a grand façade, and wings at either end. The entire building, with the exception of the mullions and quoins, is of mellow, age-old red brick, and with its high-pitched roof of tiles and its axe-hewn oaken beams, is a sheer delight to the eye of the beholder. Not easily, even in a country noted for the beauty of its ancient buildings — something, alas, that future generations will never be able to say of the present monstrosities erected in this benighted age — can Grandchester Manor be matched for loveliness and charm.

Felix Heron brought the car to a smooth halt in front of the heavy oaken front door, and almost before the car had ceased to move, Benson the butler came down the worn stone steps to greet them. He was not at all in keeping with the house. No old retainer this, but a youngish, active man, dark-featured and dark-haired, with a thin face and high cheekbones.

'Sir Richard is expecting you, sir,' he said with a hint of a cockney twang, as he opened the door of the car. 'He's in the library. He asked me to take you to him as soon as you arrived.'

Heron got out and was followed by Thelma. They followed the butler into the big hall with its ancient, and now faded, coats of arms, and were ushered into a long room, the black oak-panelled walls almost completely hidden by countless books.

Sir Richard Alperton, lean, still straight-backed, and with the tan of many years spent under a tropical sun, came forward with a smile of pleasure.

'So good of you both to come in answer to my wire,' he said in a deep and pleasant voice. 'A terrible thing happened here in the early hours of this morning.'

'I saw the constable at the gate,' said Heron, 'and guessed that something pretty serious had occurred.'

'You're right,' replied Alperton. 'I have some people staying here. One of them, a man named Norman Cassell, was found stabbed to death in the Tudor Garden.'

★   ★   ★

Felix Heron looked at the worried face of the man before him and pursed his lips. 'I appreciate your unpleasant position, Alperton,' he remarked, 'but why have you

9

asked my help? Surely the police . . . ?'

Sir Richard stopped him with an impatient gesture. 'The police are a lot of incompetent fools!' he exclaimed angrily. 'A bungling collection of imbeciles! They are under the firm impression that my son killed Cassell.'

Heron understood. He glanced at his wife. Her face was expressionless. She was waiting quietly to hear what else Sir Richard had to say.

'Of course the whole thing is a lot of absolute rubbish,' went on the baronet. 'Bob wouldn't hurt a fly.'

'Why do they suspect him?' asked Heron.

'Have they any reason?' put in Thelma.

'Well . . . ' Sir Richard hesitated. 'I suppose they have, in a way. But to anyone who knows Bob, it's ridiculous . . . '

'Go on,' said Felix Heron as he paused. 'Tell us what the reason is.'

Sir Richard rubbed his chin crossly. 'Bob and Cassell had a violent row yesterday,' he said a little reluctantly. 'My son uttered some stupid threats.'

'What was the row about?' asked Thelma.

'It was nothing,' answered the other, shaking his head. 'Bob's got a rather hasty temper. He says things he doesn't mean when he's angry.'

'But what was this row about?' asked Heron.

'It was over Miss Warrender.' Sir Richard frowned. 'She's the daughter of my solicitor. They live close by. Their house, Cray's Lodge, is part of this estate. Bob is engaged to Kathleen, a really charming gel, and there . . . Well, there was a bit of trouble . . . '

'Over this girl?'

'Bob accused Cassell of trying to kiss her,' said Sir Richard.

'Did he? *Did* Cassell try and kiss her?' asked Thelma.

'Yes, I believe he did,' admitted Alperton. 'I don't suppose it was anything serious — you know how these things happen. She, very foolishly, in my opinion, told Bob. But to suggest that he killed the man because of it is absurd.'

Heron was not so sure of this. He had

met Bob Alperton, and he had seen something of that young man's uncontrollable temper. 'Who told the police about this quarrel?' he asked. 'Was it public property?'

'Everybody in the house heard it,' answered Alperton. 'That includes the servants.'

'Did you have many people staying here?'

'Quite a few. Most of 'em left yesterday, before this happened. Cassell, Gordon Lyle, and Doctor Stillwater were leaving today. The police have ordered Lyle and Stillwater to stay,' he added.

'What time was the discovery made?' inquired Heron.

'Shortly after half-past six this morning,' said Sir Richard. 'Benson found the body and woke me.'

'Did you say it was found in the Tudor Garden?' said Thelma, and Alperton nodded. 'Why was Mr. Cassell out so early? Was he usually an early riser?'

'On the contrary, he was usually very late,' replied Alperton. 'He was only wearing a dressing gown over his pyjamas.'

'That's certainly queer,' remarked Felix Heron. 'Has the weapon that killed him been found?'

'No.' Sir Richard shook his head. 'Superintendent Hailsham — that's the man for this district — has been searching for it. You understand,' he continued quickly, 'that the police haven't definitely accused Bob yet, but it's easy to see that it won't be long before they do . . . '

Felix Heron was silent. He wasn't at all sure that it wouldn't turn out to be as simple as that. It wasn't unusual for a hot-headed fellow like Bob Alperton to kill a man whom he thought had insulted his girlfriend. But the time of the killing was queer. And the fact that Cassell had only been wearing his pyjamas and a dressing gown.

He looked at Thelma, trying to read in her face what she thought of it all. But he got no help from his wife. She was staring out the window. It was definitely not the type of case that interested him. At the same time, he didn't want to turn down Alperton's request for help.

He turned to the baronet and caught the anxious expression in the man's face. 'I suppose,' he said, 'that you want me to try and find out who killed Cassell, if it wasn't Bob?'

'Yes, that's just what I want,' said Alperton quickly. 'Bob didn't kill him. If you find out who did, the police won't trouble us anymore.'

'And supposing that what I find out only points more closely to Bob, what then? Are you prepared to risk that?'

'Yes, I am. I have complete faith in my son, Heron. He is incapable of stabbing a man in the back.'

'Cassell was stabbed in the back?' asked Heron sharply.

'Yes,' answered Alperton. 'If Bob killed a man he'd kill him in a fair fight. I can assure you of that.'

'I agree with you,' put in Thelma quietly. 'I'm sure that Felix is going to help you — aren't you, dear?'

Heron shrugged his shoulders. 'After that,' he remarked, 'I don't seem to be left with much choice, do I?'

# 2

'It's very good of you, Heron,' said Alperton. 'I hoped you would help.'

'You'd better thank my wife,' said Heron. 'She was the one who decided.'

'I think it's going to be interesting,' remarked Thelma. 'I've got a kind of instinct that there's quite a lot behind it.'

'What do you mean, my dear?' asked Sir Richard.

'I don't know, but I've an idea that there's something big of which this murder is only a small part. Don't ask me why. I don't know.'

'She's done this before,' Heron said, smiling, 'and she's always been right.'

'Well, I must say that I feel very much happier now that you're going to look into it,' declared Alperton. 'I daresay you'd both like a drink after your drive. We shall be having lunch in just over an hour.' He went over and rang the bell. 'What would you like?'

15

'I'd like some dry sherry,' said Thelma.

'Pink gin for me,' said Heron. 'Preferably Gordon's.'

'I'll join Mrs. Heron in a sherry,' said Sir Richard.

The door opened softly and Benson came in. 'You rang, sir?' he said.

'Bring a bottle of Findlater's Dry Fly, Benson,' ordered Sir Richard. 'And a pink gin with Gordon's. Bring some iced water, too.'

The butler bowed and departed.

'When we've had our drinks, what would you like to do first?' asked Sir Richard. 'See the place where it happened, I suppose?'

'Are the police still here?' said Heron.

'Yes. Hailsham and the Chief Constable, Colonel Whickthorne. They've taken over the small smoking room from which to conduct their inquiries.'

'Then I think I'd like to start by having a word with them,' said Heron.

Benson reappeared with a tray on which were glasses, a bottle of Dry Fly, and a large pink gin. He set the tray down on a small table and turned to his master.

'Shall I pour out the sherry, sir?' he inquired.

'No, I'll see to that, Benson,' said Alperton.

'Very good, sir. The iced water is on the tray,' said the butler, and went out.

Heron looked at the pink gin approvingly. Sir Richard poured out two glasses of sherry from the bottle of Dry Fly and handed one to Thelma. 'I think you'll find that an excellent sherry,' he said.

'It's my favourite,' she said. 'We always have it at home.'

Felix, sipping the pink gin, to which he had added a little iced water, said, 'Here's to the removal of all your worries, Alperton.'

They finished their drinks, and Alperton went over to the door. 'Now, if you're ready,' he said, 'I'll introduce you to Whickthorne and Hailsham.'

They followed him across the hall. Benson, who was standing by a large carved oak chest, shot them a curious glance as they passed him, and his eyes followed them to the door at the end of the hall.

Alperton tapped on the age-darkened oak. A gruff voice from within grunted an invitation to enter. Sir Richard opened the door and they went into a small room containing a table and seven easy-chairs. Behind the table, with an open notebook in front of him, sat a florid-faced man whose expression would have completely lacked intelligence but for the shrewdness of his small blue eyes. Near him, lounging in an easy-chair, was one of the thinnest men Felix Heron had ever seen. His thinness was accentuated by the narrowness of his head. His close-cropped hair was white, and across his upper lip was a smear of moustache of the same whiteness. Standing near the table was a respectful police sergeant, trim and dapper and expressionless.

'Sorry to butt in,' said Alperton, 'but I want to introduce Mr Felix Heron and his wife, who have just arrived. I don't know whether you have heard of Mr. Heron, but he has very kindly offered to help in the investigation of this deplorable affair.'

An icy wind seemed suddenly to blow

through the little room. Superintendent Hailsham's already florid face took on a deeper tint. Colonel Whickthorne cleared his throat, a sound that he contrived to make entirely disapproving.

Felix Heron cut in smoothly and quickly. 'I expect you consider this an unwarrantable intrusion,' he said. 'Believe me, I have no wish to do anything but help. I am often consulted by both Scotland Yard and British Security.'

'Thank you, sir,' interposed Colonel Whickthorne stiffly, 'but I have asked for no assistance in this matter. I do not think any is necessary. If I had imagined that it was, I should have intimated the fact to the proper quarter — Scotland Yard.'

Heron caught sight of his wife's face and tried not to laugh. But his lips twitched, all the same. 'Of course, you don't require any help,' he said. 'As an act of courtesy, I am sure you will not refuse to let me work with you. Anything I may discover is, of course, at your disposal. If, however, you would prefer that my wife and I conduct our own investigation, then naturally I should not feel bound to notify the police of any discoveries we might make.'

'It's your duty, sir, and that of your wife, to inform the police of anything that may help them in their investigations.'

'I quite agree,' answered Heron blandly. 'That duty, however, does not stipulate any particular branch of the police force. I should, of course, inform the proper quarter — Scotland Yard.'

Thelma turned a sudden uncontrollable laugh into a cough, nearly choking in the process. Felix had so neatly turned the Chief Constable's own words against him. She apologised quickly.

Colonel Whickthorne was not slow to perceive the drift of Heron's meaning. If he informed Scotland Yard of any discoveries he might make, the credit would certainly not go to the local people. His manner when he spoke again was much more conciliatory.

'There is no need for any kind of — er — friction between us, sir,' he said. 'I was rather incensed at Sir Richard's action in sending for you without consulting me.'

'If I wish to ask a friend to look into

this matter for me,' interposed Sir Richard, 'it's my own business and nobody else's.'

'I can understand Colonel Whickthorne's attitude,' said Heron quickly. 'Naturally, any kind of crime in this district must come under his complete control. But as I am here at your request to do what I can, it would be better if we could all work amicably together. Better results could be obtained, I'm sure.'

'In my opinion,' grunted Superintendent Hailsham, 'there's very little left to worry about.'

'Indeed?' remarked Heron. 'You have found the murderer of Cassell?'

'The line of inquiry which we are following will clear the whole thing up,' declared Hailsham. 'It's only a little evidence that we need.'

'I presume,' cut in Alperton angrily, 'that you are still under the impression that my son killed this man?'

'Nobody has accused your son yet, Alperton,' said Whickthorne.

'Not openly!' snapped Sir Richard. 'But only a fool would be blind to the line of inquiry you're taking. I realised what confounded idiots you were making of yourselves, and that's why I asked Mr. Heron.'

The colonel's thin face flushed to the colour of a ripe plum. 'We are merely going by the evidence so far,' he said stiffly. 'Your son returned home in the early hours of this morning and refused to answer Hailsham's questions.'

'And quite rightly too,' retorted Alperton. 'My son has a perfect right to refrain from answering impertinent questions concerning his movements. I should have done the same myself.'

Heron tried to pour a little oil on the troubled waters of their anger.

'You've overlooked the fact, Alperton,' he said, 'that this is a murder investigation. Everybody should be prepared to help the police to the extent of their ability. But I think that we are foolish to argue at the moment. I suppose the body has been removed?'

'After the usual routine we had it taken to one of the bedrooms,' said Hailsham. 'They should be collecting it for the post-mortem at any moment.'

'I should like to see it, if I may,' said Heron, 'and also the spot where it was found.'

'There's no objection to that, sir,' said Hailsham, after a glance at the chief constable. 'Sergeant Cripps will take you.' The dapper figure of the sergeant drew itself up stiffly.

'Thank you,' said Heron. 'Will you telephone Harry, dear?' he added to Thelma. 'Ask him to come down as soon as he can.' She nodded.

They followed Sergeant Cripps out into the hall. 'You won't be able to use this telephone, Mrs. Heron,' said Alperton. 'There's something wrong with the line.'

'I'll take the car and find one in the village,' she answered.

'Try and arrange with the local pub to put Harry up,' said Heron. 'Harry is a kind of general factotum,' he explained to Sir Richard. 'He may be useful.'

'Let him stay here,' said Alperton. 'There's plenty of room.' He excused himself from coming with them on the plea that he had some business to attend to, but Heron was sure that he was going to see his son. He turned to the waiting Cripps.

'I'd like to see the place where the body was found, first,' he said.

The stolid sergeant led the way out into the grounds. They were extensive. At the back of the house a broad sweep of gravel path bordered a trimly cut lawn which led to a terrace, and from thence, by a flight of broad steps, to a Tudor garden, complete with a sundial. Beyond this was the rosery, and beyond again, an ornamental rock garden with a lake and a waterfall, fed by a small stream that bisected the estate.

The rock garden was enclosed on three sides by a thick shrubbery, backed by a belt of trees. A smaller lawn, tennis courts and a large orchard lay on the other side of the house, and the stables and garages, together with a kitchen garden, were on the left. There were several acres of parkland that stretched away to meadows and the farm holding. Altogether, Grandchester Manor was a very lovely property. Sir Richard Alperton had been a lucky man to have acquired it on the bankruptcy and unfortunate death of the previous owner.

'This is the place, sir.' Sergeant Cripps pointed to a section of pavement in the Tudor Garden at the bottom of the steps leading down from the terrace. There was an ugly stain on the grey stone. ''E was lyin' on his face,' continued the sergeant. 'Sprawlin', as you might say, kind of spread-eagled. Gave me a bit of a turn when I saw 'im.'

'Photographs were taken, of course?'

'Oh yes, sir.'

Felix Heron gave a quick glance over the path and the steps. But the stones had recorded no marks, except that sinister stain.

Neither did the body of the dead man yield anything of value. He was a short, stoutish man, with dark hair that had thinned almost to baldness on the top of the head. The features were slightly Jewish, and the expression of the face was one of surprise. The man's death had come to him unexpectedly. The body was clad in grey silk pyjamas and a rather gaudy dressing gown. On the feet were slippers of scarlet leather.

Heron saw that there were traces of gravel and a few blades of grass on the soles. There was no question that he had been killed elsewhere and his body carried to the Tudor Garden.

'Was anything found in his pockets?' asked Heron.

'Only a handkerchief, sir,' answered Cripps.

'Did the doctor state the time of death?'

'He said round about three thirty to five,' replied the sergeant. 'He couldn't go no closer than that.'

What had induced Cassell to leave his room at such an hour and make his way to the Tudor Garden? If he had been going to keep an appointment, surely he would have dressed? The nights were still cold. He must have been in a hurry. But why?

'Was there a moon last night?' asked Heron.

Cripps wrinkled his brows in an effort of memory. 'I think there was, but I wouldn't swear to it, sir. I've got an idea there was.'

'Which room did the dead man occupy?'

'The one below this, sir.'

Heron went over to the window. It overlooked the lawn, the terrace, and the Tudor Garden. The room below would have the same outlook. If there had been a moon, the lawn and the Tudor Garden would have been clearly visible. Was that it? Had the dead man seen something from his bedroom window that needed immediate action?

If he had, *what* had he seen?

Something that was so urgent that he hadn't waited to dress before going out. Something that he had decided to deal with without rousing the house.

Something . . . or someone?

★ ★ ★

Going downstairs Heron encountered Superintendent Hailsham in the hall. 'Well?' remarked that official heavily. 'Have you found anything, sir?' Slight sarcasm behind the tone of the voice, but no expression on the bovine face.

'No, but I should like to know something,' said Heron. 'Was there a moon last night?'

He saw a flicker of interest come into the shrewd eyes. 'I see,' replied Hailsham, nodding. 'You want to know whether he could've seen anything from the window, eh? Well yes, there was a moon.'

'I suppose you've already questioned everybody in the house?'

'Yes, of course,' answered the superintendent.

'You've no objection if I have a word with them?'

'Not at all, sir. I understand that the chief constable has no objection to your co-operation.'

'Thank you,' said Heron. 'Are you leaving now?'

'Yes, sir. We've done all we can for the moment.' His manner was still a little cold but there were distinct signs of a possible thaw.

Felix Heron left him and went in search of Alperton. He found him in the library sipping a Dry Fly sherry. He seemed a trifle disappointed that Heron had not discovered anything.

'Have a drink?' he said. 'We've about fifteen minutes before lunch.'

'I'd like another pink gin,' said Heron.

Sir Richard pressed the bell. 'D'you think they'll arrest Bob?' he asked anxiously.

'Not yet,' answered Heron. 'They're holding their hand for something more definite, I think.'

'They'll wait a long time,' Alperton grunted. 'Bob had nothing to do with it.'

Benson came in answer to the summons.

'Bring Mr. Heron a pink gin — Gordon's,' ordered Alperton.

'Has my wife come back yet?' asked Heron.

'No, sir, I don't think so,' answered the butler.

'When you come back, I'd like to ask you a few questions,' said Heron.

Benson gave an almost imperceptible bow and went out.

'What's your opinion of this business?'

29

asked Sir Richard when they were alone again.

'Too early yet.' Felix Heron shook his head. 'Not enough to go on.'

Thelma came in at that moment. 'I got through to Harry,' she said. 'He's catching the next train. Miss Climp is going to look after things until we get back.'

'Good,' said Heron. Miss Climp was a woman of uncertain age but with a remarkable ability for dealing with any and every contingency that could possibly arise. She looked extremely prim and proper, with the outward appearance of a Sunday-school teacher. But this was deceptive. There was nothing in the way of vice and the sordid side of life that Miss Climp did not know. Her language, at times, would have left a seasoned Billingsgate porter speechless with envy.

'Would you like a sherry?' asked Sir Richard.

'I certainly would,' answered Thelma, and he poured one out from the bottle of Dry Fly.

Benson returned with the pink gin on a

salver. 'Thanks.' said Heron as the butler poured in a little iced water. 'Now, Benson, I expect the police have been worrying you quite a lot and I'm sorry to go over the same ground again. But I want to hear exactly what happened. How did you come to make the discovery of the murder?'

Benson cleared his throat and told them what he knew. He had risen at six, which was his usual time. It was his custom in fine weather to take a stroll in the grounds before starting his day's work. When he had come downstairs there was nobody else about except a kitchen maid. He had gone out by the front door and walked round to the back of the house, and across the lawn to the terrace. He had been horrified to see a man lying on the path in the Tudor Garden. Going down the steps, he had seen that it was Mr. Cassell. There was blood on the back of his dressing gown and he appeared to be dead. Benson had hurried back to the house and awakened Sir Richard, who had instructed him to ring the police.

He found that it was impossible to get any reply from the telephone which seemed out of action. He had wakened Sir Richard's valet and he had gone on his bicycle to the police station. Just as the man was riding away, Mr. Robert had hurried from the direction of the Tudor Garden. He was fully dressed but unshaven, and his clothes were stained and creased. He had gone straight up to his room without a word. This was the story that Benson had told the police.

'Did you hear anything during the night?' asked Heron.

Benson shook his head. 'Nothing, sir.'

'Did any of the other servants?'

'Not to my knowledge, sir.'

'Mr. Robert was coming from the Tudor Garden — is there an exit from the grounds that way?'

'There's a path leading to a gate that opens on the main road, sir.'

'There's nothing else you can tell me at all?'

Benson shook his head again. 'No, sir.'

Heron let him go.

'What do you think of that?' demanded Alperton.

'I think it was very foolish of your son not to have explained to Hailsham what he was doing out so early and where he had been,' said Heron.

Before Sir Richard could reply, the luncheon gong boomed through the house.

* * *

In the sombre dining room Felix Heron made the acquaintance of the other people in the house. Grouped at the long refectory table were three people, one of whom was known to Heron and his wife: a thin, angular woman who was Sir Richard's sister-in-law. Her name was Agatha Hughes and she acted as house-keeper. He and Thelma had met her on their previous visit.

The other two were men. Dr. Stillwater was a very large man with almost white hair and a straggling beard. He was dressed so carelessly that he was almost slovenly, his jacket stained and crumpled and stretched to the point of bursting the buttons, over his enormous girth. Gordon Lyle, in contrast, was small and fair. His clothes were neat and of the latest fashion. A colourless man with practically no eyebrows.

'Dashed unpleasant business, eh?' he remarked in a rather affected drawl when Alperton introduced Felix and Thelma and explained why they were there. 'How long d'you think it will be before we're allowed to go?'

'That's a matter for the police,' said Heron.

'Bob is acting like a complete fool!' said Agatha Hughes in her high, thin voice. 'There is no reason why he couldn't have explained why he went out and where he had been.'

This coincided with Heron's own opinion, but he made no comment. A deep rumbling growl reached his ears, and he realised that Dr. Stillwater was speaking. It was rather difficult to understand that slurred voice, but he gathered that Stillwater was inquiring if he had discovered anything.

'I'm afraid not,' he answered. Did they think that he worked by some magical process of his own? He'd only been there for a short while.

Benson, assisted by a trim maid, served soup and thin slices of crisp toast. 'In my opinion Cassell was killed by a burglar,' remarked Lyle. 'He got up for some reason during the night and saw a stranger prowling about the grounds and went out and accosted him. Plucky thing to do! More than I would!'

'Have you any reason for suggesting that?' asked Heron. 'Did you see or hear anything?'

'Good Lord, no!' said Lyle quickly.

Dr. Stillwater emerged from a splashing of soup to say in a deep rumble, 'Slept as sound as a bell — always do!'

'I thought I heard something,' volunteered Miss Hughes. 'I mentioned it to that man, Hailsham, but he didn't seem very interested.'

'What did you hear?' asked Thelma.

'It sounded like a shot,' answered Agatha Hughes. 'I may have been mistaken. I was half asleep.'

'What time would that be?' inquired Heron.

'No idea,' she said. 'About three o'clock perhaps.'

'Can't have had anything to do with this business,' grunted Alperton. 'Cassell was stabbed, not shot.'

'How far away was this sound you heard, Miss Hughes?' asked Heron.

'It sounded quite near.'

Felix Heron let it drop, but he made a mental note all the same. If there had been a shot it was worth investigating. Apart from this, nobody had heard anything at all during the night. There was nothing strange about this. Cassell could quite easily have left the house without making any sound.

There was nothing to be gained by further questions, and he began to talk about a number of things that had no connection with the murder. In spite of his efforts, however, there was a gloom over that luncheon table that refused to disperse. Heron was glad when the meal was over.

Coffee was served in the drawing room,

a long and lovely room that extended the entire length of the house with windows either end, and furnished with some really beautiful pieces of antique furniture. A restful room of soft colours and some fine and delicate watercolour drawings.

Felix drew near to Thelma as they entered the room. 'Any luck?' she murmured.

'No, it's a complete mystery at the moment,' he whispered. Turning to Sir Richard, he said aloud, 'Do you think I could have a word with Bob?'

'I don't know why he didn't come to lunch,' replied Alperton, frowning. He said to Benson, who was setting out the coffee things on a low table before Miss Hughes, 'Go up to Mr. Robert and ask him to come down. Tell him Mr. Heron would like to see him.' Benson departed. 'You'll find him a little difficult,' he said. 'I don't know what's got into him.'

'Why has he adopted this extraordinary attitude?' asked Heron.

'Obstinate young ass!' said Agatha Hughes. 'Black or white?'

Lyle, Felix, and Sir Richard elected for

black coffee. The rest had white.

'He's been very irritable lately,' said Alperton. 'One of his worst moods.'

'You've always spoiled him,' said Agatha Hughes, splashing hot milk into the coffee cups. 'Help yourselves to sugar.'

Benson came back. He looked rather unhappy. 'Mr. Robert refuses to leave his room, sir,' he announced. 'He told me to say that he'd no intention of answering any stupid questions and that he'd like to be left alone.'

Sir Richard Alperton's tanned face darkened. 'I'll go and speak to him — ' he began angrily, but Heron stopped him.

'Don't,' he said quietly. 'If he's determined to adopt this attitude, it won't do any good.'

'Mr. Robert has locked himself in, sir,' put in the butler.

'The young fool!' growled Alperton. 'What the deuce is making him behave like this?'

'Dashed silly thing to do,' said Gordon Lyle.

'It's worse than silly,' retorted Felix

Heron. 'If he wanted to be arrested for murder he couldn't go a better way about it! Well, we shall just have to wait until he comes to his senses. Tell, me,' he went on, changing the subject, 'what do you know about Cassell? Who was he and how long have you known him?'

It was Alperton who answered him. 'I met him through the Warrenders,' he said. 'I haven't known him very long — about three months, I think. When I bought this estate, I wanted one or two alterations made. Warrender said Cassell knew the place well and might be able to help.'

'How did he know the place well?' interrupted Felix.

'Cassell was private secretary to the previous owner,' replied Sir Richard. 'That was Bannister, Francis Bannister, the fellow who went smash over that washing machine company.'

'Bannister? Didn't he die in a motor car accident?'

'That's right.' Alperton nodded. 'If he hadn't been killed he'd have gone through the bankruptcy court. His affairs were in a shocking state. He was hopelessly insolvent. This house was put up for sale by the official receiver, and I bought it.'

'I remember, there was quite a stir at the time,' said Heron. 'So Cassell was his secretary, was he?'

'Yes, and he was hoping to be mine, I think,' said Alperton. 'He hinted at it more than once. But I wasn't too struck with him. I had nothing against him, you understand. I just didn't like him very much, that's all. He was always pleasant and well-behaved, except for that business with Kathleen Warrender. I shouldn't have asked him here, only . . . Well, he practically begged to come.'

'I did not like him,' growled Dr. Stillwater from somewhere in the depths of his being.

'Didn't know much about the fellow,' said Lyle.

'Where did he live?' asked Thelma.

'He had a small flat in London,' answered Alperton. 'He used to live here, of course, when he was working for Bannister.'

Heron drank his coffee and put down

the empty cup. There didn't appear to be anything in this that bore on Cassell's death, but it was only by collecting everything that was known about him that a possible motive might come to light. Of course, there was always the chance that the police were right and Bob had killed the man. But that stab in the back . . . ?

There was a sudden commotion in the hall. Benson, white of face, burst into the room.

'Sir Richard,' he cried, 'will you see the gardener from Cray's Lodge?'

'Why should I see the gardener from Cray's Lodge?' demanded Alperton crossly.

'It's Mr. Warrender, sir,' answered Benson. 'He's dead!'

'Dead?' Felix Heron broke in sharply. 'When did he die?'

'I don't know when, sir,' said the agitated butler. 'Watson has only just found the body in the shrubbery.'

'The shrubbery? What shrubbery?' broke in Sir Richard.

'At Cray's Lodge, sir,' said Benson. 'Mr. Warrender is dead, sir. He's been shot!'

41

# 3

Was this the explanation for the shot that Miss Hughes thought she had heard during the night? Felix Heron looked at Sir Richard, who was staring at Benson as though the butler had suddenly gone mad.

'I think we'd better see this man, Watson,' said Heron. 'Where is he?'

'He's in the hall, sir.'

'Then bring him in!' ordered Alperton curtly. 'Good God! What is going on round here?'

Nobody answered.

Watson, the gardener, was a small, nervous, elderly man with grizzled hair. He looked scared and frightened. In his hands he carried a stained and faded hat which he twisted this way and that.

'Now, what's all this, Watson?' asked Sir Richard. 'You say that Mr. Warrender's dead?'

Watson found difficulty in speaking. He

42

gulped twice, cleared his throat, and then replied in a shaky voice, 'I found 'im in the bushes. There was blood all over 'is face an' an 'ole in 'is forehead. Give me a fair scare, it did.'

'Yes, yes, I'm sure it did,' agreed Alperton. 'Have you told Miss Kathleen?'

'I don't think she's at 'ome, sir,' said the gardener. 'I tried ter make someone 'ear but I couldn't, so I come straight on 'ere.'

'You did quite right,' said Alperton. He frowned. 'What can have happened to Kathleen?'

'We'd better go over to Cray's Lodge,' said Heron. 'No,' he added as there was a general movement, 'only Sir Richard and my wife. The rest of you stay here, please.'

His voice was serious. This second murder, if it was murder, suggested that there was something much deeper than he had at first supposed. Cassell might have been killed by Bob Alperton in a fit of temper, but surely there was no reason for his killing the father of the girl he was engaged to?

'Come and show us where you found

Mr. Warrender,' he said to the frightened gardener.

With Watson leading the way they went across the lawn to the terrace and down the steps into the Tudor Garden. Through this and the rosery was the quickest way to Cray's Lodge, and presently they came to a little gate almost hidden by dense shrubbery which opened on a narrow lane. Turning to the left, they followed the lane for about fifty yards. It ended at the entrance to a short drive. The house, a small building with a red tiled roof, was visible from here, the drive was bordered by rhododendron bushes, and near the house the gardener pointed to the right.

'In there!' he whispered.

Heron could see nothing except that the earth by the bushes was churned up by footprints. 'Keep clear of those,' he warned, and going a little further along entered the shrubbery at a different point.

In a little clearing in the midst of the thick bushes he came upon the body of a man. He was lying face upwards, his big face a mask of half-dried blood which had come from a small hole in his forehead. He was fully dressed and over his suit was a raincoat.

Heron called to Sir Richard. The baronet came carefully and peered down over the other's shoulder. 'Yes, that's Warrender,' he said. 'Poor fellow! Who could have done this?'

Heron moved closer to the dead man. Arthur Warrender was a stoutish man of medium height with rapidly greying hair. His mouth was slightly open as though he had been on the point of uttering some cry at the moment the bullet had crashed into his brain.

'We'd better send Watson for the police,' he said, 'and we ought to get a doctor here as soon as possible.'

'I'll tell him,' said Alperton. He backed away out of the bushes. As soon as he had gone, Felix Heron made a quick search of the dead man. His fingers dipped quickly into the pockets of the raincoat and the suit beneath. He found nothing of any interest. A movement behind him made him turn quickly.

Thelma had edged her way beside him.

'Found anything?' she asked. He shook his head. 'Somebody was very busy during the early hours of this morning,' she remarked.

'Yes, somebody certainly was.'

'But not Bob Alperton?'

'It could be, you know,' said Heron. 'We don't know enough to say, do we? We don't know anything really — except that whatever happened during the night left two dead men behind.'

'One shot and one stabbed. That's curious.'

'Yes. If they'd been killed by the same person, you'd expect that the same weapon would have been used, wouldn't you?'

'Yes, I can't imagine why not.' She wrinkled her nose thoughtfully. 'I think we've got mixed up in something very unusual, Felix.'

'I agree, dear. Now look, will you stay here and wait for the police while I go up to the house with Alperton and see why that gardener didn't get any answer?'

He turned as Sir Richard came back. 'We'll go up to the house, Alperton,' he said. 'I want to know if everything's all right.'

'You don't believe that ... ?' Sir Richard broke off. 'Surely nothing can have happened to Kathleen?'

'Anything can happen,' said Heron.

There was no visible sign of life to be seen when they reached the house. Felix Heron rang the bell long and loudly.

No reply.

He rang again and knocked loudly.

Still no reply. No sound at all from within the house.

'There doesn't seem to be anyone in,' he said.

'I don't understand it.' Alperton frowned. 'What can have happened to Kathleen and the servants?'

'Let's try the back,' said Heron. He walked round to the rear of the building. He tried the handle of the back door. It was locked, and rapping on the knocker brought no more reply than had his knocking and ringing at the front.

Felix Heron felt uneasy. His face was serious as he looked at Sir Richard. 'We'll have to try and get in somehow,' he said.

'I don't like this silence at all.'

He began to look for some way of getting in. There was a small window a few yards away from the back door and his lips compressed as he looked at it. Somebody had already used it for the same purpose as he was contemplating. The putty around a pane of glass had been removed and the pane taken out. It was resting against the wall below the window. The sill was white with the dust from the putty. He pointed this out to Alperton.

'Do you mean there's been a burglary?' Sir Richard goggled at him in surprise.

'Let's hope it's nothing more serious,' said Heron, and the other gasped. The window was of the casement type and swung open when he pulled it. Before climbing in he made sure there was nothing to be learned from the dust on the sill. There was the mark of a knee imprinted in the powdered putty and it was possible to see the criss-cross pattern of the cloth of the intruder's trousers. Heron pulled himself up on to the sill and squeezed through the narrow window, dropping gently into the room beyond.

It was a scullery, and facing him was a half-open door. It led to a small, well-fitted kitchen. For a moment he stood listening but there was no sound from inside the house. It was completely silent. He found his way round to the back door and unlocked it.

'The place seems to be quite deserted,' he said as Alperton joined him inside. 'However, we'll soon make sure.' He closed the back door and led the way along a passage that ran from the kitchen to the square hall. A clock ticked softly but otherwise there was absolute silence.

'Anyone about?' called Heron, but there was no reply to his hail.

'It's extraordinary!' muttered Alperton. 'I don't understand it.'

Felix Heron looked round the hall. It was comfortably furnished. A brown fitted carpet covered the floor and the few pieces of furniture were of the best quality. Two doors on the right stood half-open and going to the first of these, Heron looked in.

His exclamation brought Sir Richard

quickly to his side. 'What is it?' he demanded.

Heron pointed to the room beyond the door. Normally it had been used as a study; that was evident from the large desk and the bookshelves. At the moment it looked as if it had been hit by a cyclone. The carpet was littered with a mass of papers which had come from the empty drawers of the desk. These had been pulled out and turned upside down on the hearthrug. The books had been tumbled haphazardly on the floor on the floor and the door of a small safe stood open, its contents scattered round it.

'What the deuce has been happening here?' grunted Sir Richard, his eyes almost popping from his head.

'Somebody's been very busy,' said Heron, looking at the mess with interest. 'Don't go in!' He laid a warning hand on Alperton's arm as he was moving forward. 'We'll make a closer inspection presently. Let's see the rest of the house first.'

He pulled the door shut, being careful not to touch the handle, and went to the other room on this side of the hall.

It was larger than the study, and furnished as a comfortable lounge. Here the search had been continued, though not to such a great extent. A small writing desk had been treated in the same way as the other. The contents of the drawers lay scattered on the floor. A rack containing papers and magazines had suffered in a similar way. Everything that contained papers or any kind of small objects had been thoroughly searched. This was not the result of an ordinary burglar. Whoever had broken into Cray's Lodge during the night had been looking for some special object.

There were two other rooms on the ground floor, the dining room and the drawing room, and these also had suffered at the hands of the searcher.

What had the intruder been looking for?

★   ★   ★

Felix Heron was intensely interested. What at first might have been something very ordinary had become a problem after his own heart. He left the rooms as they were and continued to explore the rest of the house.

With Alperton at his heels, muttering his amazement at what they had discovered, Heron mounted the thickly carpeted stairs to the landing above. It was the same shape as the hall, and the upper rooms were immediately above those below. The doors, however, were all shut. Choosing the first, Heron wrapped his hand in his handkerchief, twisted the handle, and flung the door open.

Beyond was a daintily furnished bedroom, and the bed was occupied! The figure of a girl in silk pyjamas was lying on the crumpled bedspread, her face half-hidden by a towel that had been bound round her mouth. Her wrists and ankles were secured by strips torn from a sheet which had been thrown down in the middle of the room.

Heron went to the bed, and two large and very frightened eyes stared up at him.

'Kathleen!' exclaimed Sir Richard. 'Who did this? Are you hurt, child?'

In a few seconds Heron had removed the gag and freed her mouth, but she couldn't speak. Her throat was so dry that her efforts were almost inaudible.

There was a carafe of water and a glass on a side table, and splashing some of the water into the tumbler, Heron supported the girl's head on his arm and held the glass to her lips.

She drank, thirstily and gratefully.

'Where's — where's Father?' she managed to gasp at last.

'He's not here at the moment,' answered Felix quickly, before Alperton could speak. 'How did this happen, Miss Warrender?'

She swallowed with difficulty. 'It was . . . the man,' she replied weakly.

'What man?' asked Sir Richard.

'I don't know who it was,' she answered. 'I only saw him dimly in the dark. He was bending over the bed . . . '

'What happened then?' said Heron, busy with the strips that bound her wrists and ankles.

'I was going to cry out but he pressed on each side of my neck, and I don't know what happened after that . . . '

'What were the servants doing?' asked Sir Richard. 'Surely they would have heard?'

'The servants aren't here,' she said. 'Father sent them away yesterday.'

'Sent them away?' echoed Alperton. 'Why?'

'I don't know. He just said they could have a holiday.'

'Has your father ever done such a thing before?'

'No, never. I thought it was funny.'

'When are they supposed to come back?' asked Heron.

'This afternoon,' she answered. 'Where's Father?'

'Tell me more about this man.' Heron had freed her and she stretched her cramped legs.

'I can't tell you much,' she said. 'I was asleep when he woke me.'

'How long had you been asleep?'

'Not very long. Something woke me before. I don't know what it was — it was something sharp and loud, that sounded quite near. I listened but I couldn't hear anything else. I thought I must have dreamed it.'

The noise she had heard, thought Heron, must have been the shot that had killed her father.

She was looking at him curiously. She had been away when he had been at Grandchester Manor before, and she was obviously wondering who he was.

'How — how did you manage to find me?' she asked.

Alperton looked embarrassed. It was difficult to explain without telling her about her father. Heron came to the rescue.

'It's difficult to explain now,' he said. 'It's a long story.'

'You're keeping something from me,' she broke in. 'What is it? Why isn't my father here?'

There was no help for it. She would have to be told. In a few minutes the police would be here. Better to tell her now.

'I'm afraid you must prepare yourself for a shock,' said Felix gravely. 'While you've been lying here helpless two very serious crimes have been committed. Some time during the night Norman Cassell was murdered.'

The back of her hand went up to her mouth. Her face whitened and into her eyes crept a look of fear. 'Norman — murdered?' She whispered the words. 'How . . . who — who killed him?'

Heron guessed the reason for her anxiety. She was thinking of Bob Alperton. 'We don't know yet,' he said. 'The other . . . tragedy affects you more closely.'

'You mean — father?' she said huskily.

'Yes. He was shot in the shrubbery near the house. The police will be here soon.'

She stared at him. Her face was white, but she was too stunned for tears. 'That . . . must have been the sound that woke me,' she said almost to herself. 'The shot. That what it was — a shot!'

'Yes, I think it was,' said Heron.

'Where's Bob?' She turned suddenly to Alperton. 'Is he all right?'

'Yes, yes, my dear,' answered Sir Richard, 'of course, he's all right.'

The sigh that left her lips was one of

relief. She had expected something different, thought Heron. Had she expected that he was under arrest? Did she think, too, that he had killed Cassell?

'If you feel strong enough,' he said, 'perhaps you could get dressed? The police will want to see you.'

'I'm perfectly all right,' she said. 'I'll dress and come down.' They left her and closed the door.

'What the devil is at the back of all this?' demanded Sir Richard. 'What was the reason for all that mess downstairs and the attack on that poor girl . . . ?'

'Something very queer,' said Heron.

'Well, it exonerates Bob; that's something. Even a fool like Hailsham can hardly suspect him of this.'

Heron didn't answer. He was not at all sure that it did exonerate Bob Alperton. That abrupt question from the girl concerning him had been very illuminating — and the anxiety and fear in her eyes that had accompanied it.

She was afraid, and her fear was for Bob. Why?

★ ★ ★

When they reached the hall, Heron suggested that Sir Richard could go and take Thelma's place. His wife would be of more help in the house. Sir Richard could wait for the police.

Alperton wasn't at all eager to go, but he reluctantly agreed. When he had gone, Heron began his examination of the lower rooms. He had just finished the dining room, which was the least disturbed, when Thelma arrived.

'I was wondering what had happened when you were so long,' she said. 'My goodness! What a mess!'

'Wait till you see the other rooms,' said her husband. 'You'd think a herd of elephants had been through the place.' He led the way into the drawing room. 'Look at that!'

Thelma's eyes widened. 'Good gracious, what's the idea?' she asked.

'You can ask that again,' Heron said. 'This is nothing to the study. That's *really* in a mess! Let's see if we can find any traces of the intruder and why he intruded.'

They set to work. Long practice had enabled both of them to make a search of a place with speed and accuracy. But they found nothing.

They came at last to the study, and Thelma gasped when she saw the state it was in. 'He didn't leave a stone unturned, apparently,' she said.

'Or an avenue unexplored,' grunted Heron. 'He was determined to find something. What this special object is, I've no idea. I wish I had. It's probably the hub of the whole thing.'

'Do you think he found it?'

Heron shrugged his shoulders. 'It's impossible to judge, isn't it?' he said. 'We don't know if there's anything missing or not.'

'The girl might be able to help,' said Thelma.

'Yes. She shouldn't be long before she's dressed. Let's get on with it, anyway. I'd like to get finished before the police get here. They won't be best pleased if we disturb the place too much.'

They began a rapid search of the room. The safe had been opened with the key.

The bunch still hung from the lock. The intruder must have taken it from Warrender after he shot him.

If any confirmation were needed that it was no ordinary robbery, it was found in a packet of notes that lay among the chaos on the floor. Fifty-six pounds in pound notes. There were a number of legal documents and bank statements, a cheque book, but nothing of interest until Thelma called her husband over to show him a scrap of paper she had found. It was quite small, little bigger than an inch and a half. It had been torn from a larger sheet, and words had been scrawled on it in pencil.

Heron peered at it with interest. ' . . . ird St,' he read aloud. 'H'm, might mean anything.'

'Turn it over,' said Thelma.

He did so. On the back was part of a word. 'Ban . . . '

'It looks as though it was torn from a notebook. Could it be important?'

'I don't know. Possibly. It's the only thing we've found, anyway. We'll keep it.' He put it away in his pocket-book.

Kathleen Warrender came in. She had dressed in a dark grey suit. Her face was still pale but she was quite calm and composed.

'I've made some tea,' she said. 'I was dying for a cup . . . Good Heavens, what a mess!'

'Perhaps you can help,' said Heron. He introduced Thelma. 'Can you tell us if there's anything missing?'

She looked helplessly at the disorder and shook her head. 'How can I?' she asked. 'I knew nothing of Father's papers.' She looked from one to the other. 'Are you connected with the police?'

Felix Heron explained his position.

'I see. Would you like some tea?'

Her voice was quite steady and they were rather surprised that she was so little outwardly upset by what had happened.

'I should,' said Thelma promptly.

'Do you mind coming into the kitchen?' said the girl. 'I thought I'd better have it there.'

'You did quite right,' said Heron. 'We mustn't disturb anything until after the police have been.'

She led them out into the neat kitchen.

On the table she had set a tray with cups and saucers. While she was pouring the tea, Heron asked her, 'Did your father have a large practice?'

'He didn't have a practice at all,' she answered. 'He'd retired. Didn't you know that?'

'No. I understood that he dealt with Sir Richard's legal affairs.'

'Oh yes, he did that,' she admitted. 'But that was all. After Mr. Bannister was killed and father had attended to the winding up of his affairs, he retired.'

'Was he Francis Bannister's lawyer?' asked Heron with sudden interest.

She nodded. 'Yes. I believe father had a great deal of trouble over the bankruptcy. I don't know much about it but he grumbled quite lot over the hopeless mess Mr. Bannister's affairs were in. Do you both take sugar?'

'Please,' Heron answered a little absently. He was thinking that at last there was something that seemed to link up. Arthur Warrender had been Francis Bannister's solicitor, and he was dead. Norman Cassell had been Francis

Bannister's private secretary, and he was dead, too. There must be more than a coincidence in this. Both these men had been closely connected with Bannister, and both of them had been murdered.

And there was another thing. Why had Warrender retired at such an early age? He couldn't have been more than fifty-six or -seven. It was unusual for a solicitor to give up his practice at that age. He put his thoughts into words.

'I've often wondered the same thing,' said Kathleen. 'When Father told me he was retiring I told him I was surprised. He said that he'd made all the money he wanted, and it was stupid to go on working. He was always fond of the country and so he bought this house.'

'When did he buy it?' asked Heron.

'About three months ago,' she answered.

'That was practically at the same time that Sir Richard Alperton bought Grandchester Manor,' said Thelma.

'It was just before,' said the girl.

And Grandchester Manor had belonged to Francis Bannister, thought Heron. Curious. Almost immediately after Bannister's death his solicitor had retired and bought a house that was part of the estate. He remembered the 'Ban . . . ' on the scrap of paper. Was that part of the name 'Bannister'?

Things were beginning to gel, but there was a long way to go yet. And it was fatal to go too fast. It was so tempting to twist facts to suit a preconceived theory. He had so few facts at present, even to twist into anything, he thought ruefully. Still, there was a glimmer where there had been complete darkness.

There was a heavy step in the hall. Going to the kitchen door, he opened it and looked along the short passage.

Superintendent Hailsham had arrived.

# 4

'So you're here before us, eh?' remarked Hailsham as he saw Felix Heron. 'I hope you haven't disturbed anything, sir?'

'Everything is exactly as I found it,' answered Heron.

'This has developed into a very serious business,' said the superintendent, 'very serious indeed. Not only has Mr. Warrender been shot dead, but his house has been broken into as well.'

'Yes,' agreed Heron.

Hailsham eyed him shrewdly. 'It seems to me that this burglary may account for the murder of Mr. Cassell,' he went on. 'If there's a desperate criminal in the district, that might be the solution.'

'Up to a point I agree with you,' said Heron. 'It seems that whoever killed these two was desperate. But I don't agree that he was a professional burglar.'

Hailsham raised his eyebrows. 'Oh, what makes you say that, sir?'

Felix explained his reasons, and Hailsham was obviously impressed. 'There's a lot in what you say,' he admitted. 'It doesn't help very much, does it?'

'Not at all,' said Heron. 'It only makes it more difficult. No burglar would have overlooked that money, and few professional crooks would have made such an infernal mess.'

'But if robbery wasn't the motive, sir,' said the superintendent, drawing down his heavy eyebrows in a frown, 'why did he break in?'

'He was looking for something,' answered Heron. 'I can't even suggest what it was, but it was something special.'

'That seems to be probable, sir. And we can't say whether he got it or not.' He turned his eyes in the direction of Kathleen Warrender, who had come with Thelma into the hall. 'It's a pity you didn't see more of this man, miss. You can't think of anything that would help us to identify him?'

She shook her head. 'I only saw him for a moment, and my room was nearly completely dark.'

At Hailsham's request she repeated what she had already told Heron.

'You've no idea why your father sent the servants away, miss?' he asked, frowning.

'None at all. He'd never done such a thing before.'

'Can you suggest what this man was looking for?'

'No. I've no idea.'

'Was your father expecting anyone?'

'He didn't say anything about it.'

'Had there been any difference in his behaviour lately?'

'He'd been a little worried during the past week or two,' she said after a pause. 'I asked him if there was anything troubling him but he said no.'

'I see,' said Hailsham, and then: 'I believe you're engaged to Mr. Robert Alperton, miss?' She nodded. 'Was your father friendly with Mr. Alperton?'

'Yes, very.' She looked surprised.

'Your father didn't object to your engagement?'

'No, he was very pleased.'

Hailsham pursed his lips. Obviously he

had been trying to find some way of connecting Bob Alperton with both the murders. He was reluctant to give up his original theory about the Cassell murder, but unless he could find a plausible motive in the case of Warrender it would be difficult to proceed with the case against Bob Alperton.

He put one or two more questions to the girl on the same lines, but he failed to gain any further evidence that there might have been a rift between Bob Alperton and her father. Eventually he gave it up. 'I won't bother you any more now, miss,' he said, and she went back to the kitchen.

'Well,' Hailsham remarked, 'I don't mind admitting that I'm fairly puzzled.'

'We're all in the same boat,' said Heron. 'It seems that we shall have to discard our original idea,' went on the superintendent. 'Unless, of course, we can find a link between these two dead men that would supply a motive for Mr. Alperton having killed 'em.'

'In face of this new development, I think you'll be wasting your time if you

68

bother any more with Bob Alperton,' said Heron.

'His attitude has been very peculiar, all the same, sir,' said Hailsham.

'He's behaving as you would expect a man of his stature to behave,' said Heron. 'Bob Alperton is one of those people who resent interference. He dislikes being pushed around, so he digs his toes in the ground and becomes stubborn.'

'I can understand that — up to a point, sir. But I can't understand why he couldn't explain where he'd been when he was asked. He was away from the house for the greater part of the night and only returned in the early hours of the morning. Where did he go?'

He stopped as Kathleen came back quickly. 'There's a man over by the wood,' she said a little breathlessly. 'I was upstairs and I saw him from one of the windows. He looks as if he was watching the house.'

'What is he like?' asked Thelma.

'Like a tramp,' said the girl. 'Dirty and ragged.'

'Let's have a look at him,' broke in

Heron. 'Which window was it you saw him from?'

'The back staircase window,' she replied. 'We can go this way.' She led the way up the main staircase and along a short passage to a window at the top of a narrow staircase that was for the use of the servants. 'Look!' she exclaimed. 'There he is now!'

They crowded round the window. Beyond a low hedge that separated the grounds of Cray's Lodge from a belt of woodland, a man was walking impatiently up and down, stopping every few seconds to gaze anxiously at the house. His clothes were old and shabby and growth of dark stubble showed up against his pale face. He seemed to be expecting someone.

'Is there any way of reaching him without going across the garden?' asked Heron quickly.

'You could go out through the main gate,' she answered. 'It's a short distance along the lane to a little footpath that will bring you to the wood.'

'Come on,' said Heron, and ran down

the main staircase with Hailsham and Thelma at his heels. He opened the front door and hurried round to the drive. Sir Richard was talking to a constable near the spot where they had found the body of Arthur Warrender. They ignored him and the little group and ran down the drive to the main gate.

They found the footpath but they could see nothing of the man, for the path took a sharp turn. But as they rounded this bend they saw him. Unfortunately he saw them at the same moment.

Giving them a sharp glance, he turned abruptly and plunged into the wood. Felix and Thelma ran after him, followed by the panting superintendent. But the trees and the undergrowth grew thickly, and their quarry had a fairly good lead. They could hear him crashing through the bushes and weeds, but they caught no further sight of him. They continued on until they came to a clearing, and stopped to listen. But now there was no sound at all from the man they were pursuing.

'We've lost him,' panted Heron. 'Damn!'

'It's a pity he caught sight of us,' said

Thelma. 'It gave him too much of a start.'

'I wonder who he was?' grunted Hailsham.

'I'd very much like to know,' said Heron. 'Both who he is, and what he was doing hanging about here.'

'Perhaps he was just a tramp?' suggested his wife.

'Perhaps,' said Felix. 'But I don't think he was.'

★  ★  ★

They retraced their steps to Cray's Lodge and were greeted by Sir Richard Alperton with a frown. 'Where the deuce did you go tearing off to?' he demanded irritably.

Heron explained and Alperton's frown deepened. 'Must've been a tramp,' said Sir Richard.

'I don't think so, sir,' Hailsham disagreed. 'He wasn't behaving like a tramp.'

'He was waiting for something, or someone,' said Thelma. 'It looked as if he'd come there to keep an appointment.'

'That's what I thought,' said Felix.

'Who with?' asked Alperton.

'Well, it might have been with Warrender,' said Heron.

'If he was waiting for Warrender, sir,' put in Hailsham, 'then he couldn't have known he was dead.'

'It's not much use conjecturing, is it?' said Heron. 'Come here, Hailsham. Look at these marks in the earth. There are two different sets of footprints. One set was made by a broad, heavily made shoe, and the other set is more elegant. I think these are Warrender's prints.'

'I'll check up on that, sir,' Hailsham said. 'We'll get casts made. See that these marks are not disturbed, Cowley.' The constable nodded stolidly.

'The body was in the middle of those bushes,' Heron went on, 'but I don't think Warrender was shot there. He was dragged there after he was dead. If you look here, you'll see where he was dragged. Over here, on the gravel of the drive, are one or two spots of blood. That's where he was actually shot.' He pointed out the traces to Hailsham.

'I expect you're right,' said the

superintendent. 'I'll leave my examination of the body until after the doctor's seen it; he should be here at any moment.'

Thelma, who had wandered away along the drive, called to them: 'Felix, come here!' They went and joined her. She pointed to a patch of shrubbery on the other side of the drive. 'Look there!' she said.

Something was lying at the foot of one of the bushes, almost hidden by the leaves. It was a thin-bladed knife, the blade discoloured by brownish stains.

'You'd better take charge of that, Hailsham,' said Heron. 'I'd say it was the weapon that killed Cassell!'

The superintendent carefully picked up the knife with his handkerchief wrapped round his hand. It was a very ordinary knife, a kitchen knife, but the blade had been ground to razor-sharpness. 'This is beyond me,' grunted Hailsham, staring at the weapon. 'How did it get here?'

'The murderer must've brought it,' said Heron. 'He came here after he'd killed Cassell. Warrender met him in the drive and he shot him.'

'Why shoot him?' demanded Hailsham. 'Why not stab him, if he had the knife with him?'

'Your guess is as good as mine,' said Felix.

'I'll have this thing tested for prints,' said Hailsham, wrapping the knife up carefully in his handkerchief and stowing it away in his breast pocket, with difficulty because of its length.

'I doubt if you'll be lucky,' remarked Felix. But he was wrong.

The handle of the knife was to yield evidence which, though it cleared up one aspect of the mystery, rendered the rest more puzzling.

★ ★ ★

The tinkle of a bicycle bell heralded the arrival of the doctor. Dr. Yarde, the police-surgeon for the district, was a round, ruddy-faced little man with a weather-beaten complexion that testified to many hours spent in the open.

He slid off his machine as he reached them. 'Got a message that there'd been another death,' he said. 'Is that right?'

'Mr. Warrender's been shot,' said Hailsham.

'Warrender? Good Lord! How did it happen?' cried the little doctor.

'It was murder,' said Hailsham, and the doctor gaped at him.

'Two murders in a few hours! We'll be in the Sunday papers! Where is he?'

The superintendent showed him. Giving his bicycle to the constable to hold, Dr. Yarde plunged into the bushes, taking care avoid the footprints in the earth. They heard a lot of muttering from the bushes, interspersed with several grunts, and presently the little doctor came back, brushing earth and dead leaves off his clothes.

'He couldn't have known what hit him,' he stated. 'Dead before he even reached the ground! Bullet went straight through his temple into the brain. Still there. There's no exit wound.' His small, twinkling eyes flickered from one to the other. 'What's going on round here?' he continued. 'Is there a lunatic at large? We'll have the whole district in a panic if this goes on.'

'I shall be surprised if these murders are the work a lunatic,' remarked Heron. 'They are all part of a carefully contrived plan, in my opinion.'

'And who are you, sir?' asked Dr. Yarde. Hailsham explained.

'Oh, I see. H'm! Well, I hope you get to the bottom of this business soon. Don't like it — don't like it at all! It's not pleasant to have a killer loose about the place, eh? Have the body taken to the mortuary, Hailsham. I'll get the bullet out and let you have the P.M. report. Bye, everybody. Got an enormous visiting list.' He grabbed his bicycle from the constable, scrambled to the saddle, and was off down the drive as fast as his fat legs could pedal.

'I think I like Dr. Yarde,' remarked Thelma.

'He's good at his job,' said Hailsham.

'I think it would be a good idea if you took Miss Warrender back with you, Alperton,' suggested Heron. 'The servants will be back soon, but she's bound to feel — '

'Of course,' broke in Sir Richard. 'The

poor child must be very upset. I'll go and ask her now.'

He went off towards the house and Heron turned to Hailsham. 'I suppose you'll be staying here?' he said, and when the superintendent nodded: 'If you find any prints on that knife, you might let me know.' Hailsham nodded.

Heron made no mention of the scrap of paper Thelma had found. He wanted time to look at it more closely. If it turned out to be anything of importance, of course he would tell Hailsham all about it.

When they got back to Grandchester Manor, the rest were having tea in the drawing room. Kathleen, who seemed glad to be there, had been given tea and sandwiches and was being fussed over by Agatha Hughes, who seemed to be genuinely fond of the girl.

Heron had a cup of tea, and then with an excuse went in search of the butler. 'Where is the telephone, Benson?' he asked.

'In the library, sir. But it's not working.'

'I know. I want to have a look at it.'

Benson gave him a rather strange look as he walked away.

The telephone stood on the desk by the window, and he quickly found that the instrument was quite dead. There was no sound at all when he put the receiver to his ear. Heron traced the flex from the telephone to the bell on the wainscot. There was no break in it. The line from the bell ran out at the side of the French window, and going out, he followed the course of the wire up the brickwork. And he soon found why the phone refused to work. The lead-covered wire had been neatly cut!

Someone, for reasons of their own, had wished to cut Grandchester Manor off from the rest of the world. The question was — who?

# 5

Harry arrived soon after tea. Felix introduced him to Sir Richard and Agatha Hughes, and was secretly amused at the impression Harry's appearance seemed to make on both of them. They tried to conceal their astonishment but were not entirely successful. However, Harry was conducted to his room by an equally astonished Benson, and after a wash had an interview with Heron.

Felix Heron briefly put the secretary in the picture, telling him exactly what had happened in the short time he and Thelma had been at Grandchester Manor. Harry listened with the closest attention. He had a remarkable memory and Felix knew that every detail he had been told would be filed away in his mind, to be brought out when it was required. Harry never needed to take notes. He was the human tape recorder.

Dr. Stillwater and Gordon Lyle were

strolling about the lawn, looking rather at a loose end. Quite obviously they resented the fact that they were not allowed to leave. Of Bob Alperton there was no sign at all. He remained locked in his room. Benson had taken up his lunch on a tray and been curtly told to leave it outside the door. Bob had eaten it, as the empty tray testified.

Kathleen was talking to Thelma. She appeared a little distressed at his attitude, but not so much as Heron had expected.

Leaving Harry to amuse himself, Heron went up to the room that had been allotted to him and Thelma. Pulling an easy chair up to the open window, he lit a cigarette and settled down to think.

The murder of Arthur Warrender, and what had happened at Cray's Lodge, had altered the original problem drastically. Cassell was now part of a larger pattern. Heron marshalled what few facts he had collected. They were disappointingly meagre. What had taken Cassell to the Tudor Garden in the night? Whatever it was, it had been unexpected. From the window of his room he had seen something, the sight of which had sent him post-haste out into the grounds.

What had he seen?

Round about the same time, Arthur Warrender, fully dressed, had been lurking about the drive at Cray's Lodge. What had he been doing? Why had he sent the servants away? What reason had he had for wishing Cray's Lodge to be empty that night except for himself and his daughter? Who was the unknown man who had tied up Kathleen and ransacked the house?

These were questions without answers. There was not enough data to answer them. The only common denominator, as yet, was Francis Bannister.

Cassell had been his secretary, Warrender had been his solicitor. But Bannister was dead; he had died in a car crash. Heron decided that the circumstances of the accident would be worth enquiring into more closely. It was a job that Thelma could do well.

But there were still other questions to be considered. The identity of the man who looked like a tramp and who had run away at Cray's Lodge. The extraordinary attitude of Bob Alperton and the reason for his nocturnal expedition. The deliberate cutting of the telephone wire so that no message could be sent over the line from Grandchester Manor. Were these all part of the problem? Heron was pretty sure they were. It was absurd to suppose that there was more than one plan in operation. No, all these things represented part of the whole sinister fabric.

He lit another cigarette and took from his pocket the scrap of paper Thelma had found in the disordered study. It was definitely part of the page from a notebook, but what did it mean? What did ' . . . ird St' stand for? The name of a street? That was possible. Was the 'Ban . . . ' the beginning of the name 'Bannister'? That was possible, too. But what good were possibilities? He wanted certainties.

There came a tap at the door, and Benson came in. 'Superintendent Hailsham's asking for you, sir,' said the butler. 'He's downstairs.'

'Ask him to come up here,' said Heron. He carefully put the scrap of paper back in his wallet. A few minutes later Hailsham came in.

'Sit down,' said Heron. 'I thought we should be more private here. Hope you don't mind.'

'I prefer it, sir,' said Hailsham. 'You asked me to let you know if we found any prints on that knife.'

'And you did!' broke in Felix excitedly.

'Yes, there were several very clear prints indeed,' answered Hailsham.

'Whose?'

Hailsham lowered his voice. 'They were the prints of the dead man, sir,' he said, 'Arthur Warrender!'

Heron looked his surprise. 'Arthur Warrender's!' he repeated. 'You're quite sure?'

'Oh yes, quite sure. They are the only prints. And it was the knife that killed Cassell.'

'You've confirmed that?'

Hailsham nodded. 'There's no doubt. It exactly fits the wound. Dr. Yarde is prepared to swear it was the weapon.'

'It looks as though it was Warrender who killed Cassell.'

'It certainly does, sir, but who the dickens killed Warrender?'

Heron got up and paced the room. 'It fits with what we know,' he said. 'Warrender, for some reason or other, stabs Cassell, and is returning home when he meets this other man. Startled, he throws the knife away, and the other man shoots him. The unknown man drags the body into the bushes, breaks into the house, ties up Kathleen Warrender, and conducts his search.'

'For what?' demanded Hailsham. 'For what, Mr. Heron?'

'If we knew that we'd have the answer to the whole business,' answered Heron. 'You've put a guard on the place?'

'Cray's Lodge, sir?'

'Yes. If this man didn't find what he wanted he might come back. He might even be that fellow, the tramp, we saw hanging about.'

'Surely he wouldn't risk that, sir?'

'He's risked a lot already, hasn't he?'

'Well, Cowley is on duty there. He'll be

relieved later, and there'll be a man on duty all night.'

'I should warn your guard to be careful.'

'Do you think there's any danger, sir?'

'I most certainly do. This man has killed once; he won't hesitate to kill again if it's necessary. Of course, there may be no need for him to come back. He may have found what he was after the first time.'

'I'll see that my men are warned,' said Hailsham.

'By the way, the servants came back, but they couldn't tell us anything.'

'Are they at Cray's Lodge?'

'No, I sent 'em back to their home in Oxford. They're a married couple, name of Wilton. They were surprised when Warrender sent 'em away. He gave them no reason, just told them to clear out until the following day.'

'I wonder why he did that?' murmured Heron.

'Wanted the place to himself, I suppose.'

'But he didn't have it to himself,' said

Felix. 'His daughter was there.'

Hailsham shrugged his broad shoulders. 'As I said, the whole business is queer.' He dragged a massive watch from his pocket and looked at it. 'I must be getting along. I've got an appointment with the chief constable. He's not going to be any too pleased with my report.'

'He thought it was simpler than it's turned out, didn't he?' said Heron.

'Yes — so did I, for that matter. I was pretty sure it was young Alperton.' He went over to the door. 'If you get hold of anything, sir, I hope you'll let me know.'

'I shall do nothing without your co-operation,' promised Heron. 'I may make one or two inquiries on my own, but I'll let you have the results as soon as I know them myself.'

Hailsham departed.

It was getting on for dinner time when Heron went down. He found Alperton in the library by himself, sipping a Dry Fly sherry. 'Do you know where my wife is?' asked Felix.

'She's somewhere with Kathleen,' replied Sir Richard. 'Would you like a drink?'

'I'll join you in a sherry,' said Heron. 'By the way, you needn't worry any more about Bob. The police have given up the idea that he had anything to do with Cassell's death.'

'Well, that's good news, anyway,' said Alperton. He finished pouring out a Dry Fly and brought the sherry over to Heron. 'I'm infernally grateful to you, Heron.'

'I don't think I had much to do with it,' said Felix. 'They'd have come to the same conclusion after Warrender's murder, in any event.'

'I still wish I knew what the matter is with Bob,' said Sir Richard. 'I can't understand the young ass! He remains shut up in his room and won't speak to anyone. Even Kathleen can't get anything out of him.' He gulped the remainder of his sherry angrily. 'How long will they keep Lyle and Stillwater here, d'you think?'

'I've no idea,' answered Heron. 'Everybody's still under suspicion, you know. Tell me, what do you know about Warrender?'

'In what way?'

'Generally. What sort of man was he?'

'He always struck me as a pretty good chap. Actually, I know very little about him, except in business. I can't tell you very much, I'm afraid.'

Dinner was a dull and boring meal. Afterwards Sir Richard, Agatha Hughes, Stillwater and Lyle played bridge. Thelma talked to Kathleen until the girl pleaded that she was tired and went up to bed. Bob did not put in an appearance at all but, according to Benson, ate an enormous meal which was taken up to him on a tray.

Heron was glad when the evening was over and he was able to go to bed. For a little while he and Thelma discussed the issue, and then his wife fell asleep. But he was not so lucky. His mind niggled away at the problem without getting anywhere. He heard the clock below strike twelve, one, half-past one . . .

He was just on the point of dropping off to sleep when he heard a sound that brought him back to complete wakefulness. A soft and stealthy footstep was passing along the passage outside the bedroom door. Somebody was up and active in the sleeping house.

Who?

*    *    *

Without waking Thelma, Felix Heron slid gently out of bed, dressed quickly over his pyjamas, pulled on his shoes, and softly opening the door stepped out into the corridor.

No sound came to his ears now, except the gentle ticking of the clock in the hall. And then he heard a faint movement from below.

It hadn't been his imagination. Somebody was about.

He moved silently along the passage to the head of the staircase, and looked down. A gleam of light flashed for a second, flashed again, and then shone steadily. The person below was using a torch.

Heron began to creep cautiously down the stairs. The house was old but the solid oak beneath his feet did not creak. They built well in those days. He could see no one yet, but the light flickered hither and thither. There came the faint rattle of a chain and the rasp of a bolt. A cold wind blew up towards him. The front door had been opened!

The light went out and a soft thud reached his ears. The night prowler had gone out! He hurried down the rest of the stairs and fumbled among the overcoats on the hallstand for his own. It was dark in the hall, but he found it by sense of touch and pulled it on. Opening the front door, he slipped out, closing it gently behind him.

The night was cloudy but a watery moon filtered faintly through the wispy veil of cloud, and the light it gave was enough to enable him to see a dim figure hurrying across the lawn to the terrace. Heron went quickly in pursuit.

Who was it who had gone out at such an hour, and where were they going?

The man he was following went down the steps into the Tudor Garden and disappeared from view. Heron moved quickly in his wake, praying that he wouldn't look round until he reached the cover of the terrace. But the other seemed in too much of a hurry to worry about being followed. Along the paved path, through the arch and into the rose garden he hurried. Was he making for the gate to the lane that led to Cray's Lodge? It looked very much like it.

The man disappeared through the gap in the shrubbery and Heron slowed down a little to give him time to get ahead. There was no doubt that he was making for the lane; but presently, when Heron came out of the gate, there was no sign of him.

For a moment he thought that the other had eluded him. And then he saw him walking quickly ahead. He could see that he was carrying something that looked like a suitcase. He made no effort to go to Cray's Lodge but went on past the entrance.

Heron frowned. Where was the man going?

He got his answer almost at once. The other turned off into a footpath that bordered the edge of the wood. It was very dark here. The trees grew thickly, and although only beginning to leaf, obscured what little light the moon gave.

The man he was following never hesitated. He walked rapidly towards the spot where the tramp had plunged into the wood when he had been scared off. Heron lost sight of him. But he could still hear the noise he made forcing his way through the undergrowth.

The night was very silent, and he had to move with the greatest caution in order that he should not give himself away to the man in front. What had brought him to this gloomy wood at such an hour? And what did the suitcase contain?

They came to a clearing in the trees, but the other did not stop. He hurried on into the thick woodland beyond.

Was he running away, whoever he was? Was that the reason for the suitcase? Was this a short cut to a railway station?

This part of the forest was denser than the rest, and the undergrowth was thicker and more closely tangled. It was difficult to force a way through. Heron tore his hands on trailing brambles — and then, suddenly, the sounds of the other's progress ceased!

And then he heard the mutter of voices. The man who had left Grandchester Lodge had come to meet someone!

Felix was certain that he was on the verge of an important discovery. He must move warily. It would be fatal if his presence were suspected. With infinite care he edged forward and came at length to a second and larger clearing. At one side of this was a dilapidated wooden shack that at one time had probably been a keeper's hut. A faint light shone from the dirty window, apparently from a candle by its dimness. The murmur of voices continued from inside the crazy structure.

Who was he talking to? The tramp?

Heron was determined to find out. He advanced as silently as he could over the rank grass. The moon had come out from the filmy cloud, and its light filled the clearing. If they looked out the window or came out, he was bound to be seen.

But the murmur of voices continued, and in three seconds more Heron was crouching by the wooden wall of the hut. They were talking in very low tones and he could not distinguish anything that was said. He raised his head carefully until he could apply an eye to one corner of the window. It was so dirty that he found it difficult to see anything very clearly.

The hut seemed empty except for a broken box on which had been stuck a candle. Beside the box was an open suitcase, apparently containing food. Across the improvised table, facing each other, were two people, one holding in his hand a bottle of beer.

One was Bob Alperton, and the other was the ragged, bearded tramp!

# 6

Although he had expected the tramp, Heron was not prepared to see Bob Alperton. What had he in common with the dirty, unshaven man who was ravenously stuffing bread and meat into his mouth which had obviously been brought him by his visitor? Who was this ragged man who lived in the crazy hut in the wood? Was it here that Alperton had come when he had been seen returning in the early hours of the morning? It seemed more than probable. But why couldn't he have explained? Did these two share some guilty secret that had made it impossible for him to tell?

Felix Heron slid gently away from the window into some nearby bushes. The thing to do was to keep an eye on the tramp. There was no point in following Bob anymore. He would, presumably, return to the manor. It was the tramp who was important.

It was not a very cheerful prospect. The night was cold and the ground was damp. He fervently hoped that he wouldn't have a long stay. It was a pity he couldn't hear what they were talking about. That might have supplied him with all he wanted to know, but all that reached him was a muffled rumble. The only thing to do was to wait!

It was over half an hour later when the door of the hut opened and Bob Alperton came out, followed by his scruffy companion.

'It's damned good of you, Alperton,' said the tramp gratefully, and his voice was the voice of an educated man.

'Oh, rubbish!' retorted Bob. 'You've got enough grub to last you until I come along tomorrow night. I'll come at the same time. Oh, I nearly forgot these.' He pulled a packet of cigarettes out of his coat pocket.

'I suppose it's safe?' said the tramp dubiously.

'For you, or for me?' asked Bob.

'For both of us.'

'You needn't worry about me. I can

97

take care of myself,' said Bob. 'I don't see why you should worry, either. Nobody passes this way. You're all right for a day or two. I'll get things fixed up by then.'

'I shall never forget this, you know, old man.'

'Bilge!' said Bob. 'Don't forget tomorrow at the same time.'

He set off across the clearing and was soon lost in the wood. The tramp stood in the doorway of the hut for a moment, and then went inside, closing the door behind him.

Heron breathed a sigh of relief. Here was an answer to his immediate problem. There was no need to keep a cold vigil. Bob Alperton's words proved that the tramp was not likely to leave before the following night at any rate.

Heron waited to give Bob time to get well ahead, and then began to retrace his steps through the wood. He didn't hurry because he had no wish to catch up with Bob Alperton. It would need a lot of explaining and spoil the whole thing. Bob would know he had been followed and certainly warn the man in the hut.

He emerged at last by the hedge which bordered the footpath and divided the fringe of the wood from the grounds of Cray's Lodge.

And as he reached it he heard the sound of a shot!

It was followed quickly by two more, and they came from the direction of the house!

There was a light in one of the lower windows, and as he vaulted the boundary hedge and began to run across the lawn he saw another light spring up as the door was opened. Running footsteps came pounding towards him, and a figure loomed up in his path. He heard a snarled imprecation and a pistol exploded almost in his face!

He leapt at the man and received a blow in the chest that sent him staggering. By the time he had recovered his balance, the shooter was scrambling over the hedge.

Heron went after him but the other turned and fired again. He felt a sharp pain on the left side of his head, and he almost fell. He tried to recover himself but his legs were suddenly weak, and the blood from the wound in his temple was blinding him.

It was useless to try and catch the unknown now. Pulling a handkerchief from his breast pocket, he tried to staunch the blood, and began to walk unevenly towards Cray's Lodge. As he reached the still-open door of the house a bulky figure staggered into view. It was the constable who had been guarding the place. The man was wounded, for blood streaked his face. In one hand he grasped a heavy army revolver, and as he caught sight of Heron he levelled it at him.

'Put your 'ands up!' he growled hoarsely. 'Go on, quick!'

'It's all right,' called Heron. 'What's been happening here?'

'Never you mind what's been 'appening!' snarled the constable. 'You stand still an' put up yer 'ands, or I'll put a bullet in yer!'

'Don't be a fool! I'm Felix Heron.'

'I don't care if yer the Shar of Persia,' shouted the policeman. 'You just try comin' any closer . . .'

'Oh, all right!' Heron was getting irritable. That revolver in the hands of the incensed constable might prove extremely dangerous. With his hands up he moved forward into the light that streamed out from the door. The constable eyed him with anything but a friendly expression.

'Was you the feller that tried to pot me, just now?' he demanded.

'No,' snapped Heron. 'I was on my way back to the manor when I heard shots. I came to see what was happening and a man shot at me.'

''Old on, sir,' broke in the policeman. 'I remember you now. Very sorry, but I wasn't taking no risks.'

'That's all right,' said Heron, lowering his hands. 'What did happen here?'

He followed the constable into the kitchen. The man put the revolver down on the table, pulled out a handkerchief and mopped his blood-stained face. 'That feller tried ter take me by surprise,' he explained. 'I'd just 'ad a bite to eat an' a cup o' coffee, an' I was sittin' here, when before you could say 'snap' an 'and come

101

out of nowhere like an' tried ter press something over me face. I pulled it away an' jumped up. There was a feller in a dark kind o' raincoat, with a scarf over 'is face, just be'ind me. Lord knows 'ow he got there! I 'adn't 'eard a sound, but there 'e was an' 'e was holding this pad what reeked of some drug. I went to tackle 'im, but he pulled a gun from 'is pocket an' fired point-blank. The bullet grazed the top o' me 'ead an' sent me 'alf silly. He took to 'is heels an' I fired a couple o' shots after 'im. Then everything went sort o' queer for a bit. I was tryin' ter get a bit of air when I see you. Lummy, I don't want no more of it!'

'You didn't hear anything until the hand came over your mouth?' asked Heron.

'Not a blessed thing. 'E must've moved like a cat.'

'Let's have a look at your head.' Heron led the man over to the light. The bullet had ripped a narrow strip of skin and hair from the constable's head. Little damage had been done but it had bled profusely. It was a wonder the shock of the impact hadn't put the man right out, but he looked a tough specimen, and his skull was probably pretty thick.

'Go and wash that under the tap,' said Heron. 'If we can find something, I'll bind it up.'

'What about you, sir? That's a nasty gash at the side of yer 'ead.'

There was a mirror near the sink and Felix inspected his injury. It was only a graze along the side of his head. Both he and the constable had been very lucky tonight.

He went through into the hall, switched on the light and made his way up the stairs to the bathroom. Here in a wall cabinet he found a first-aid box and, carrying this back to the kitchen, he dressed the constable's wound and then got the man to dress his. When this was done, he began a search for any traces of the intruder. He found a thick wad of cotton wool, still wet with chloroform, lying by the chair in which the policeman had been sitting when he was disturbed. How the man had got in was quickly discovered. The window beside the back door had not been repaired and he had used that.

The communicating door between the scullery and the kitchen had been open, and the policeman had been sitting with his back to it. It had been easy.

The constable's description of his assailant was vague. He was a man of medium height and slight build. But further than that the constable couldn't go, because the man's face had been concealed by the scarf. One thing, however, was certain: he couldn't have been either Bob Alperton or the tramp. And that was a concrete fact. It was something at least.

It seemed fairly certain that the unknown man had come back to find the thing, whatever it was, that he had failed to find in his previous search. And it must be something that was pretty important for him to take such a risk.

Heron stayed for a little while longer with the constable before he set off to return to Grandchester Manor. 'I don't think you'll be disturbed again,' he said reassuringly before he went. 'I'll suggest to Superintendent Hailsham that he arranges for a double guard in future.'

When he got back to the manor he was faced with a problem. The front door was shut fast and he had not allowed for this contingency. Of course, Bob had fastened it when he returned. Felix rubbed his chin and considered what to do. If he roused the house it would advertise to Bob that he had been out, and that young man couldn't fail to be suspicious. In which case he would find some means of warning his companion of the hut in the wood. There would be no meeting on the following night and that would upset Heron's plans.

Perhaps he could find an unfastened window that would solve the problem. He made a slow circuit of the building but every window was secure. He came back to the porch. There seemed nothing for it except to arouse someone to let him in.

And then a thought struck him. Thelma! He would throw a pebble up at the window of their room. She could come down and open the front door.

And at that moment the front door opened!

He heard a startled exclamation and found himself staring into the astonished face of Gordon Lyle!

# 7

The surprise was mutual. Lyle was evidently completely taken aback at seeing anyone there at this hour of the night. 'Who is it?' he demanded sharply.

'It's Heron, Mr. Lyle,' replied Felix. 'Are you suffering from insomnia?'

The man was fully dressed, even to the extent of his overcoat and hat, and he carried a suitcase in his hand. 'What are you doing here?' asked Lyle suspiciously.

'Just strolling about,' said Heron.

Lyle's eyes went to the bandage round his head. 'What's happened?' he asked. 'Hurt yourself?'

'I had a little argument with a man who preferred bullets to words. Unfortunately I had no means of retaliation.'

Lyle drew in his breath quickly. 'Do you mean someone shot you?' he asked.

'That's right. Luckily he wasn't a very good shot! Where are you going with that suitcase, Mr. Lyle?'

'That's my business!' snapped Lyle. 'It's nothing do with you.'

'It's got a lot to do with me,' retorted Heron. 'Listen! Tonight another attempt was made to enter Cray's Lodge. The constable on duty was attacked. He wasn't seriously hurt, luckily. His assailant, who was armed with a gun, wore a scarf round his face, so we haven't got a description of him. He got away after shooting at me. Now I find you up and dressed . . . '

'Are you suggesting that I'm the man who shot at you?' snarled Lyle angrily.

'No, I'm merely saying it's peculiar. Perhaps you would like to explain?'

'Why should I?' demanded the other. 'This is supposed to be a free country.'

'That is a delusion under which most people suffer,' replied Heron. 'About the only thing free is speech, and that is subject to the law of slander. Come, Mr. Lyle. The police have requested that no one should leave here. You weren't thinking of leaving, were you?'

Lyle hesitated. When he spoke his tone was more conciliatory. 'Since you've caught me,' he said, 'I suppose I may as well admit it. Look, I've got a very important appointment in the morning. So I thought I'd clear out before anyone could stop me. That's the truth.'

It was a good story, thought Heron. Was it true? There was no means of telling. Lyle could have made it up on the spur of the moment.

'You'd better reconsider going,' he said. 'You'll find yourself in serious trouble if you do. You might even find yourself arrested.'

'There's nothing against me,' broke in Lyle, but his pale face was alarmed. Heron noted that his usual rather affected manner of speech had gone.

'You'll be giving them something, won't you?' said Heron. 'They'll jump to the conclusion that you know a great deal more about this business than you've admitted.'

'Look, it's essential that I should be in London in the morning,' declared Lyle earnestly. 'It means a tremendous lot to me — a large amount of money. Why should I lose this for something that I really had nothing to do with?'

There was a lot in what he said, if it were true. 'Listen to me,' said Heron. 'You go back to bed. I'll see Hailsham in the morning and try and get his permission for you to go. I can't promise that he'll agree.'

'I say, will you really?' said Lyle. 'That's awfully decent of you, Heron. What time will you see Hailsham?'

'As soon as possible in the morning.'

'That's fine.' Lyle was jubilant. 'I do appreciate it, Heron — really I do.'

'Well, let's go to bed,' said Heron. 'I don't want to rouse the house.'

Cautiously they closed the front door and shot the bolts. At the top of the stairs they parted, with a whispered goodnight.

Thelma was still fast asleep when Heron crept into the room. Obviously she had heard nothing of the excitement of the night.

Felix was very tired and his head ached from the wound. Silently and quickly, he slipped out of his clothes and slid into bed. In less than three minutes he was asleep.

'What on earth have you done to your head?' demanded Thelma when their early-morning tea woke them. 'What have you been up to?' She sat up in bed and inspected her yawning husband. He stretched himself and gulped some tea.

'I've had quite an exciting night,' he said with a grin, and proceeded to tell her all about it. Thelma listened with interest.

'Well, I do think you're mean!' she exclaimed when he had finished. 'Why didn't you wake me before you went after Bob Alperton?'

'There wasn't time,' he answered. 'Anyway, you were fast asleep.'

She examined the wound in his head critically. 'I'll bet that's pretty sore,' she said. 'I'll dress it properly when you've had your bath. What do you make of all this?'

He finished his tea and put down the cup. 'It wants a lot of thought,' he answered. 'The chap in the hut is our first consideration. We've got to find out who he is and what he's after.'

'Well, he's certainly someone who Bob knows very well,' remarked Thelma. 'And you should get an answer to both your queries tonight. What about this man in the scarf?'

Heron shook his head. 'Unknown quantity,' he said. 'There's something he wants pretty badly at Cray's Lodge.'

'What?'

'You can answer that one just as well as I can.'

'I can't answer it at all,' she declared.

'That's what I mean,' retorted her husband.

'Do you think Lyle was speaking the truth?' Thelma asked.

'Yes, I do.'

'Are you going to ask Hailsham?'

'Yes, but I shall also suggest that he puts someone on to follow him. This affair is so obscure that we can't afford to take any risks. Until we know what it's all about, there's no saying who's mixed up in it.' He swung himself out of bed and pulled on his dressing gown. 'See you in a few minutes, dear,' he said, cheerfully, and made his way to the bathroom.

When later they went downstairs, they found that they were the first up. Benson was hovering about the sideboard and greeted them respectfully as they sat down to breakfast. Sir Richard joined them halfway through the meal. He was not at his best in the morning. He had little to say and looked gloomy and liverish.

At a few minutes after eight, Heron set off for the police station. He found that Hailsham was already in possession of the facts concerning the attack on the constable at Cray's Lodge. 'You were right, sir,' he said. 'I'll have two men on duty tonight.

'I was going to suggest that,' said Felix. 'Now, listen! I've got a lot to tell you. He launched into an account of the night's events in detail, and the superintendent listened wide-eyed.

'This beats the band!' he declared. 'We must find out who this feller is.'

'We'll do that tonight, with luck,' said Heron. 'Meanwhile, here's another bit of news for you.' He related his encounter with Gordon Lyle and the man's excuse for being up and dressed, if excuse it were, and put forward his request that Lyle should be allowed to leave.

Hailsham was a little dubious. 'It looks to me as if he might be mixed up in this business,' he said. 'He might even be the feller in the scarf.'

'It's possible,' agreed Heron. 'But we can't do any harm by letting him go to London — so long as he's trailed.'

'I haven't got a man to spare, sir.'

'Don't worry about that. My secretary, Harry, will shadow him. He's the best 'tail' I ever knew. Nobody can shake Harry off. He sticks to 'em closer than glue.'

'Oh, well in that case, sir, I suppose it'll be all right,' said Hailsham reluctantly. 'Though I must admit I don't like it.'

'Harry's outside in the car,' said Heron. 'I'll tell him to slip back to the manor and tell Lyle you've granted him permission to leave.'

He went out to the car and spoke to his secretary. 'Now,' he ended, 'you're not to let this man Lyle out of your sight. You understand, Harry?'

Harry grinned, an awe-inspiring sight that had put fear into the hearts of strong men. 'You can trust me,' he said, and Heron knew that he could do just that.

He re-joined Hailsham in the latter's office. 'I've another suggestion to make,' he said. 'Can you find out how many strangers have appeared in this district, say within a radius of fifteen miles, recently?'

'What's the idea, sir?'

'It would be a good idea to check up. If you find someone who's recently come here, find out all about him. If you do find anyone — '

'Then we're dealing with someone who's been here all the time, sir,' said Hailsham shrewdly.

'Exactly. It won't do a lot of good, but it'll help. Now, about tonight,' said Heron. 'I'd like you and I to handle the tramp. I'm going up to London this morning, but I shall be back in time to follow Bob Alperton, or wait for him near the hut.'

'Why wait for tonight, sir?'

'I want to catch them together,' said

Felix. 'I've an idea we shall learn more that way.'

Hailsham was forced to agree, and Heron walked back to Grandchester Manor. Gordon Lyle had already gone and with him had gone the redoubtable Harry. He made an excuse to Sir Richard that he had to go to town on business, but would be back that evening; and leaving Thelma to deal with anything that might happen during his absence, he set off in the car for London. His intention was to probe into the affairs of the late Francis Bannister in the hope that he would find a clue to the mystery.

His hope was to be partially realised, for in the history of the dead man he came across two facts that eventually were to lead him to the truth.

merely a symbol. 'Bannister, as you probably know, dealt in colossal amounts. His liabilities are enormous. His own fortune had gone completely. It is not that that we are dealing with. It is a matter of two hundred thousand pounds that cannot be accounted for in the company's funds.'

'That's quite a respectable sum,' said Heron. 'It's missing, is it?'

'Let us say ... unaccounted for,' corrected Mr. Thompson cautiously. 'We are still working on the accounts. It may be found.'

Felix leaned forward. 'Such a sum as that would provide exactly the motive both I and the police are looking for,' he said seriously. 'If someone is under the impression that this large amount is concealed somewhere, and that Warrender and Cassell knew where ...'

'They both assured me,' interrupted Mr. Thompson, 'that they had no knowledge of what had happened to this sum.'

'Somebody may have thought that they did know.'

# 8

Felix Heron reached his flat in Park Lane soon after eleven. There were several things that had accumulated during his short absence but Miss Climp had dealt with most in her usual efficient manner.

After a cup of coffee, he put through a call to the offices of *The Megaphone*. He asked to be connected with the news editor and in a few seconds was talking to that harassed man.

'The name of the man who handled the Bannister business,' repeated Mr. Latham. 'Hold on, will you? I'll ring you back.'

Heron hung on. He and Latham were old friends and he knew that any information he wanted would be given him if it were possible.

'Hello?' said the telephone after a few minutes. 'The man you want is a chap named Thompson. You'll find him at Bankruptcy Buildings, Carey Street. What have you got hold of, Heron?'

'I don't know yet,' said Felix.

'Well, don't forget the old firm if it's anything good,' said Latham. 'Bannister's still news.'

'I won't forget you — and thanks,' said Heron.

A minute later he was on his way to Carey Street. He located Mr. Thompson, who turned out to be the senior official receiver. He was a thin, grey-haired man with glasses and a permanent expression of unhappiness, due most probably to his job.

'I don't know that I should be justified in disclosing any details of the late Francis Bannister's affairs,' he said in a thin, reedy voice. 'What authority have you for asking?'

'Frankly, none,' answered Felix candidly. 'I am investigating two murders which were committed in Oxfordshire during the past thirty-six hours. I am following up what I believe may put me on the track of the murderer.'

Mr. Thompson pursed his thin lips. Gently he pushed his glasses more firmly on his thin nose. 'You are under impression that Bannister's bankrup — or rather insolvency; he died before was actually adjudicated — has a bearin on these two crimes?'

'Yes, I do. The two people concerned were closely connected with Bannister during their lifetime.'

'Who were these people?'

'Norman Cassell, Bannister's secretary, and Arthur Warrender, his solicitor,' said Felix.

Mr. Thompson's face changed. He looked quite human. 'Dear me!' he exclaimed. 'I knew them well. They gave me a great deal of assistance in dealing with Bannister's affairs.'

'His affairs were very involved, I believe?'

'Involved? They were chaotic, sir! Chaotic! We had the greatest difficulty in straightening out the muddle. Even now there are certain assets that cannot be traced.'

'Involving a large sum?'

'Large is a matter of degree,' said Mr. Thompson, to whom money had become

118

119

'Everything would have been a lot easier,' said Mr. Thompson, leaning back in his chair, 'if Bannister had not died in that motor accident. He might have been able to clear the whole matter up.'

'Would it have made any difference if he had not died?' asked Felix. 'I mean, could the bankruptcy proceedings have been avoided?'

Mr. Thompson shook his head. 'No, no, quite impossible. The debts were enormous. Nothing could have saved him.'

'Not even the two hundred thousand pounds?'

Mr. Thompson laughed. It was a weird sound. 'A mere drop in the ocean, my dear sir. It would have been swallowed up by the creditors without being noticed.'

'Will you tell me,' asked Heron, 'if there was any suggestion of fraud in Bannister's affairs?'

Mr. Thompson removed his glasses. He took out his handkerchief and gently polished them. For a long time he considered before he replied. 'I can only tell you, Mr. Heron,' he said at last, 'that it was very lucky for Bannister that he died when he did.'

'Thank you,' said Heron. 'Was he aware of this?'

'That I can't tell you. Cassell and Warrender were.'

'One last question, Mr. Thompson,' said Heron. 'Had Bannister any family?'

'He was a widower,' answered Mr. Thompson. 'I don't know whether there were any children of the marriage.'

Heron went back to his flat. He felt in need of a drink, and poured out a large Johnnie Walker. Adding a little iced water, he drank it slowly. Lighting a cigarette, he sat down to ponder over what he had learned.

It was by no means certain that the missing two hundred thousand pounds had anything to do with the events at Grandchester Manor, but it was worth using as a basis for a hypothesis. Francis Bannister had obviously been aware of his impending crash. If it had only been the liquidation of his company it wouldn't have affected him so much. But it was his own private bankruptcy that had worried him. It was not unreasonable to suppose that he had salted the money away so that he would have a nice nest-egg to fall back on. This is what Thompson must have meant by fraud. Because, of course, Bannister should have turned over all his assets to the official receiver.

What had he done with the money, supposing this to be true? Was it the whereabouts of this large sum that had prompted the unknown man's search at Cray's Lodge? It was the only thing that had come to light and it was a sufficient motive for anyone. But why Cray's Lodge? Why not the manor? That was where Bannister had lived. Had Warrender had the money in his possession? It was only natural, if this were the case, that he would deny all knowledge of it to Thompson.

But there was nothing in all this to suggest the identity of the man in the scarf, from whose bullet Heron was still sore.

He poured himself out another Johnnie Walker and while he drank it jotted down some notes of the facts in his possession.

Then he went out to lunch.

During the afternoon he went down to Fleet Street and from the files of *The Megaphone* read all he could find about Bannister. What he found added practically nothing to what he already knew.

After the exertions of the previous night he felt tired and a little jaded. Going back to the flat he had some tea and, afterwards, a hot bath and changed. When he had done this he felt fresher. A stiff Johnnie Walker completed the cure, and he was ready for anything.

As he drove back to Granchester Manor and his appointment with Hailsham, he wondered what the result of the night's adventure would be.

But he never imagined in what dramatic circumstances the identity of the tramp in the hut was to be revealed.

★   ★   ★

As luck would have it he had engine trouble on the way to Oxfordshire, and this was followed by a flat tyre, so that it was nearly ten minutes past eleven when he reached the police station to keep his appointment with Hailsham. He had intended to call in and see Thelma first, but after his chapter of accidents there was no time.

He found that the superintendent had not been idle during the day. 'I followed up your suggestion, Mr, Heron,' he said. 'I've had the district combed for strangers. The job isn't finished, but up to now we've found no suspicious characters.'

'You can account for all strangers, can you?'

Hailsham nodded. 'Either friends or relations of people living here,' he said. 'It was worth trying, but nothing's turned up yet.'

'Now, I'll tell you what I've done,' said Heron, and he did so while Hailsham listened with interest.

'I believe you're right, sir,' he declared when Heron had finished. 'I'll bet this missing money is at the bottom of it.'

'It's the only tangible motive we've found as yet.'

'And it accounts for the search of Cray's Lodge,' agreed the superintendent.

'That's what this chap's after. He's looking for some record, or the actual place, where this money is hidden. Could this man Bannister have put it in the charge of Warrender?'

'I doubt if he would. Concealing assets in bankruptcy is a serious offence. No reputable solicitor would be a party to it. No, I think Bannister did this on his own.'

'What makes this feller imagine that the money might be found at Cray's Lodge, then?'

'Can't tell you,' Heron answered candidly. 'There's a good reason which we know nothing about. It's possible that Bannister made a confidant of Cassell.'

'And he told Warrender?'

'I'm not so sure about that. Remember this, Hailsham: this money, if it exists — we've no real proof of that, you know — is anybody's who can find it. Since it's already missing, nobody's likely to miss it again.'

'Just waiting to be picked up like, eh?'

'*If* anyone can find it.'

Hailsham made a gesture. 'It's a pretty involved business, sir. Let's hope tonight will clear things up a bit.'

'We shall see.' Heron looked at his watch. 'We ought to be starting, in case Alperton goes to the hut earlier than he arranged.'

Hailsham got up and fetched his overcoat. 'By the way,' he remarked as he struggled into it, 'what about Lyle?'

'I don't know yet. I haven't been to the manor. But don't worry. Harry won't lose sight of him. What about Cray's Lodge?'

'I've got two men there. If that chap comes back we'll nab him.'

'I'm afraid he won't. He'll probably guess that the place will be well guarded.'

It began to rain as they left the police station, a thin drizzle that looked as if it might get worse. It was very dark, and a cold wind swept across the country, making Hailsham shiver and turn up his coat collar. 'If we have a long wait we shall get a good soaking.' He grunted.

They walked briskly until they reached the entrance to the lane that led to Cray's Lodge, where Heron suggested more caution. 'The tramp may be on the lookout,' he said. 'If we're seen it'll spoil everything.'

Hailsham nodded, and they proceeded in single file along the little footpath which fringed the wood and bordered the grounds of Cray's Lodge. Reaching the spot where Heron had followed Bob Alperton on the previous night, they plunged into the wood and made their way in the direction of the hut.

It was slow going. They had to be careful to make as little noise as possible; but, after what seemed an eternity, they came to the clearing and in sight of the dilapidated building. There was no light now shining through the dirty window, and no sound of life from within. Only the pattering of the rain, which had increased to a heavy downpour.

Cautiously they took up their position behind the screening brambles. 'As soon as Alperton arrives and goes into the hut,' whispered Heron, 'we'll go in after him.'

The superintendent nodded and moved as a trickle of very cold water from a branch above dripped down the back of his neck. Police work was a hard way of making a living, he thought disgustedly. There were no set hours; you worked round the clock. If you were successful you got precious little praise, and if you failed you were hauled up on the carpet. Other men would be snugly tucked up in bed, instead of crouching in the cold of soaking undergrowth in the heart of a damned wood!

The time went slowly by. The chill of the rain crept into their bones, but nothing happened. The silence was unbroken except for the hiss and splatter of the rain and the rustle of the wind in the trees above.

Twelve o'clock! One! Still nothing.

And then, suddenly, Hailsham gripped Heron's arm. 'Listen!' he breathed.

Felix Heron had already heard. Someone was coming. The swish and cracking was unmistakable. They waited, almost afraid to breathe in case they should give their presence away. The sounds got nearer and nearer. They could see a darker shadow against the darkness as the figure of a man came into the clearing.

It was impossible to tell whether it was

Alperton, but it must be. It was unlikely that anyone else would be there on such a night. The man paused when he got to the middle of the clearing and seemed to be listening. Then he went on up to the hut and tapped on the crazy door. Heron saw that he was carrying a parcel and guessed that it contained more food for the tramp.

There was no reply to his knock, and grasping the rusty latch, he pushed the door inwards and squeezed himself through the narrow aperture. Evidently the door jammed on something inside and would only open a little way.

There was scrape of a match and the little window shone, dimly yellow.

'Now?' whispered Hailsham.

'No, wait.' Heron had scarcely spoken when there came a horrified exclamation from the hut. The light went out, the door was pulled violently open with a rasp of wood against wood, and the man who had entered a few seconds before came stumbling out.

'Now!' cried Heron, and jumped from behind the brambles into the clearing.

The retreating man swung round with a startled cry as he heard them. Hailsham caught him in the light of his torch as he turned, and revealed the horrified face of Bob Alperton.

'Who's that?' he cried.

'Heron,' snapped Felix. 'What are you doing here?'

'You!' Alperton's voice was hoarse. 'Oh my God, it was horrible!'

'What are you talking about?' demanded Heron. Bob Alperton, to his surprise, seemed to be glad to see him.

Bob stabbed a finger in the direction of the hut. 'In there,' he said. 'I saw him.'

'Give me your torch, and look after this fellow,' said Heron. He took the torch from Hailsham's hand and went quickly over to the hut. Stepping across the threshold, he sprayed the light over the interior.

And then he saw!

In one corner lay the huddled body of the tramp. His lips were drawn back in a grin of pain, and the front of his ragged jacket was darkly stained with the blood that had formed a little pool in the dust of the rotting floor!

131

# 9

The man was quite dead.

Heron made a swift examination and decided that he had been dead for some hours. There was a wound in the side of his neck that looked like a knife wound which, from the amount of blood, had severed one of the large arteries.

He looked round as Hailsham and Alperton appeared in the doorway. 'Look at this!' said Heron.

'My God!' exclaimed Hailsham. 'He's been murdered!'

'Stabbed in the throat,' said Heron. He shifted his gaze from the body to Bob Alperton. 'You'd better do a little explaining,' he said.

'I had nothing to do with — that,' muttered Bob. 'I found him like that.'

'I know you couldn't have stabbed him,' broke in Felix. 'He's been dead for some considerable time. Who was he?'

Bob licked his lips. 'Bannister — James

Bannister,' he said. 'Francis Bannister's son. You know, the man who — '

'I know very well who you mean,' broke in Heron. 'So Bannister did have a son, eh? What was he doing here?'

'Well,' answered Bob, 'it's a long story. Actually, he was on the run.'

'Do you mean from the police?' interrupted Hailsham.

'Yes.' Bob nodded. 'I'll tell you the whole story. There is no need to hide anything now. It wasn't my secret, you see, before; but now . . . Well, it can't harm him, poor chap.'

It was an eerie scene that lingered long afterwards in Felix Heron's memory: the dirty, draughty hut, the fixed grin of the dead man in the corner, the whine of the wind, and the drip and patter of the rain made a macabre setting as Alperton told his story.

'Jim and I were up at Oxford together,' he began nervously, steadfastly keeping his eyes away from the corner. 'That's how we became friends. I came down first and lost sight of him for a time. Then I ran across him in a night club. He had a girl with him, and he was chucking his money about. His father hadn't any time for him at all — few people knew he even had a son — but he kept him well supplied with money, though they seldom met.

'I saw Jim several times after that and we went on one or two sprees together. In spite of the amount of money he had, Jim was always in debt, but he never worried very much how he was going to get out of it. He had no idea of the value of money — it was just something to spend, and he spent it. There was this girl, too — the one who'd been with him at the night club — and she was at the bottom of his trouble.'

He paused, took out a packet of cigarettes and fumbled with a box of matches. Heron flicked on his lighter and held the flame to the end of the cigarette.

'Thanks.' Bob inhaled a deep breath of smoke and let it trickle out slowly. Then he went on. 'I hadn't seen him for quite a long time, but I'd heard all about his father's trouble and wondered how it would affect Jim. His supply of money would dry up, and goodness knew what he would do.

'Then came the accident and his father was killed in that smash. I got in touch with Jim at once and told him how sorry I was. He said things were in a pretty bad way, but he hoped he'd be able to pull through. He was gloomy, but not very worried. He was sure that enough would be saved out of the wreck to pay all his debts and save him enough to live on.

'Well, as you know, there was nothing saved. It all went to the official receiver, and even then it didn't cover old Bannister's debts.

'Dad had always liked Grandchester Manor and he bought it. Jim came to stay for a couple of weekends and was talking about getting a job. I believe Warrender had offered to help him.

'I lost sight of him again for several months, and then, one day, the day before Cassell was killed, Jim telephoned and asked me to meet him — here, in this hut.

'He sounded frantic and suggested one o'clock in the morning. I was surprised at the time and the place. I asked him to come up to the house, but he said he couldn't. He refused to say any more over the phone, but he promised to explain when he saw me. He made me promise that I wouldn't tell anyone I'd heard from him, and I didn't.'

Alperton dropped the half-smoked cigarette and put his foot on it. 'Well,' he continued, 'I kept the appointment, but I was very uneasy about it. Jim had been up to something and seemed to be in real trouble. When I got here, he was on this box smoking a cigarette and I should never have recognised him. His clothes were stained and ragged and he had a growth of beard. His face had fallen in and he looked half-starved. I could see that he'd had a pretty rough time, and what he told me confirmed it.

'His creditors had been buzzing round him like flies, but Warrender had managed to keep them from doing anything drastic. Everything would have been all right if it hadn't been for that damned girl I mentioned. Anyone could see that she was only out for what she could get — anyone except Jim, and he was crazy about her. He'd promised her a diamond bracelet for her birthday. When he hinted that now he couldn't afford it, she went off the deep end. And the fool bought the thing and paid with a cheque, knowing there was nothing to meet it but an overdraft. Of course the jewellers had taken action, and there was a warrant for his arrest. He'd been dodging the police for several days.'

'Why didn't he get in touch with Warrender?' put in Heron.

'He did,' answered Bob. 'Warrender had promised to come and see him at the hut in the morning. He couldn't come before, he said, because he had some business to attend to. I suggested that Jim should come back with me, but he wouldn't hear of it. The police might get on to him. The servants were bound to talk. If I could let him have some food he'd stay in the hut. I said I would, and that I'd try and help to get him out of his mess. I knew it was no good approaching Father; he's a stickler for strict honesty and, of course, what Jim had done was fraud, although he didn't see it that way.

He'd been so used to money that writing a cheque for anything was almost automatic. I spent most of the night in this hut and went back home in the early hours of the morning. And that's all.'

And that explained Bob's attitude. He couldn't exonerate himself without giving Jim Bannister away. But the explanation had left a bigger mystery in its place.

'You saw no one but Bannister that night?' asked Felix.

Alperton shook his head. 'No. I didn't hear anything, either. I was more surprised than anyone when I heard about Cassell.'

'Can you suggest why this man, Bannister, was killed?' asked Hailsham.

'No, I can't. I've never had such a shock in my life before as when I found him.'

'Did he ever suggest that his father might have hidden a large sum of money anywhere?' inquired Heron.

'No; is there any possibility of that?'

'I don't know . . . possibly. We'd better finish here and get away.'

They made a search of the hut, but

they found nothing to help in the identity of the murderer. The weapon had been taken away by the killer.

'There's no doubt that this is part and parcel of all the rest,' said Heron, 'though why Bannister should have been killed is beyond me.'

'And me,' grunted Hailsham. 'I thought tonight'd make things a bit clearer. It's only made 'em worse. You must've heard the shot that killed Mr. Warrender, Mr. Alperton.'

'We both heard it,' said Bob, 'and wondered what it was.'

'You didn't trouble to find out?'

'We thought it was a poacher. The sound was very faint. And in the circumstances . . . ' He broke off, but they knew what he meant.

'Did Jim Bannister know Cassell?' asked Heron.

Bob nodded. 'Of course he did. Cassell was his father's private secretary.'

'But you said he seldom saw his father,' put in the superintendent.

'He knew Cassell. Cassell used to bring him his allowance sometimes.'

'Well, I don't think we can do any more here,' said Heron. 'We can't do any good, but we ought to get a doctor.'

'I'll go back to the station,' said Hailsham. 'What are you going to do? Somebody ought to stay with the body.'

'I'll go to the police station if you like,' volunteered Bob Alperton.

'That's a very good idea,' said Heron. 'Be as quick as you can. I shall be glad to get away from here.'

Bob, looking rather relieved, hurried away.

'I don't know that we should have let him go,' began Hailsham doubtfully.

'Why not?' asked Heron. 'Come on, out with it. What have you got on your mind?'

'I'll tell you,' said Hailsham. 'I'm wondering if our first idea wasn't the right one, after all.'

'You mean . . . ?'

'That it was Bob Alperton and this feller Bannister who were responsible for the murders of Cassell and Warrender,' said Hailsham.

Felix Heron had guessed what was

coming. 'That should be sufficient answer for you,' he said, indicating the dead man in the corner. 'We were here when Bob Alperton made the discovery.'

'When he *appeared* to make the discovery,' corrected Hailsham. 'How do we know that he hadn't been to this hut before and killed him then?'

'Why should he kill him at all?'

'Because they quarrelled,' replied the superintendent triumphantly. 'Listen, my theory explains everything. James Bannister knew that his father had hidden this money somewhere. He contacts Alperton to help him find it. He thinks that Warrender and Cassell know where the money is hidden.'

'And so they kill them, effectually preventing them from divulging the hiding-place?' said Heron,

'There might have been a good reason why they *had* to be killed,' argued Hailsham. 'Then Bannister and Alperton have a row — perhaps over the division of the money — '

'Which they haven't got! I don't think much of the idea. I'm pretty sure that

Alperton was genuinely astonished to find his friend dead. Anyway, if he'd killed him before, why come back?'

'Because he'd left something behind that would incriminate him. We don't know what he may have picked up while he was in the hut alone. He was there long enough. The weapon, perhaps?'

'Why all the acting?' said Heron. 'He had no idea we were watching. Why not just slip in and get what he wanted? No, it won't hold water.'

'Can you suggest anything better?'

Heron shook his head. 'Not at present,' he admitted.'

'Bannister was the most likely person to have known about this money his father salted away.'

'We're not certain yet that this money exists. There's two hundred thousand unaccounted for, but we've no evidence to show that it was taken by Francis Bannister and hidden. He may have used it to pay some special and undisclosed creditor. That's an offence under the bankruptcy law, I know, but he might have done it.'

'I suppose you're right there,' said Hailsham grudgingly. 'But if that money isn't at the bottom of all this, what is?'

'I'm not saying that I don't believe in the existence of this hoard,' said Heron. 'I do! But we've no actual proof and I should say that it's much more likely that Warrender and Cassell knew more about its existence than Jim Bannister. He had very little to do with his father.'

'We've only Alperton's word for that.'

'Well, Thompson didn't know whether Bannister had a son, or any family, which bears out what Alperton said.'

They were still arguing the point when Bob Alperton returned with a startled sergeant, a constable, and Dr. Yarde. The fat little man was only partially dressed, and had obviously been dragged hastily from his bed.

'Are people going to be murdered round here every day?' he demanded grumpily. 'This is getting a bit too thick, Hailsham! First Cassell, then poor Warrender, and now this fellow! It's high time you put a stop to it.'

'We've got to find the person responsible first,' said Heron.

'Then you'd better hurry up,' snapped
the little doctor, 'or there won't be anyone
left alive!' Muttering under his breath, he
waddled over to the figure in the corner.
'Give me some light here,' he grunted
curtly, and Hailsham turned the light of
the torch on the dead man. Dr. Yarde
peered down. 'H'm, messy!' he commented. Kneeling down, he probed and
prodded with swift fingers. 'Killed with a
short-bladed knife. The hilt has bruised
the flesh of the neck. Carotid artery cut.
That's why there was so much blood.
Must have died pretty quickly.'

'How long has he been dead?' asked
Hailsham.

The little doctor screwed up his face.
'Four hours, could be five,' he answered.
'Can't be certain.' He straightened up,
looking curiously from one to the other.
'Any idea who did it?'

It was Heron who answered. 'No idea
at all. Probably the same person who
killed Warrender.'

'And Cassell, I suppose, eh?' grunted

the doctor. 'I'll tell you something — the people round here are getting scared. They'll be worse after this. Who is this chap?'

'His name was James Bannister.'

'Bannister, Bannister?' Dr. Yarde frowned. 'Any relation to Francis Bannister?'

'His son,' replied Bob Alperton.

'Bannister's son, eh? Never have recognised him. How did he get in this state? Suppose I'm asking too many questions. Oh, well, never mind. You don't have to answer 'em!' He clicked his teeth. 'Three murders on top of each other. The coroner's going be busy.' He yawned and blinked at Hailsham. 'Nothing more I can do now. I'll get back and finish my sleep. Thought I was going to get an undisturbed night, for a change. Better get that taken to the mortuary and put beside the other two. They'll have to build a bigger one if this goes on. Goodnight to you, what's left of it!' He disappeared into the wet darkness outside.

'Well, I'm going back to the manor,' said Felix. 'You'd better come with me, Alperton.'

'I'll be here for some time yet,' said Hailsham. 'I'll see you in the morning.'

'Yes,' said Heron, unaware that he was to see Hailsham again before the night was over. 'Come on, Alperton.'

They set off together through the dripping wood. The wind was stronger but the rain had almost stopped. They forced their way through the undergrowth in silence.

Bob appeared to be suffering from the reaction following his unpleasant discovery, and Heron had no wish to talk. There was a light in Cray's Lodge as they passed. The guard was evidently wakeful and vigilant.

They took the short cut through the little gate and the Tudor Garden. It was as they reached the terrace steps that Bob pulled up sharply.

'What's the matter?' asked Heron.

'Look there!' exclaimed Alperton.

Heron followed the direction of his pointing finger. A ladder was reared up against the side of the house.

'What in the world is that doing there?' said Bob.

146

'We'll soon see!' Heron hurried across the lawn and soon reached the foot of the ladder, which was set against the sill of an upstairs window.

'Whose room is that?' whispered Felix.

'It's empty,' began Bob, and then suddenly: 'No, it isn't. It's the room where they put Kathleen!'

# 10

Felix Heron's face was grave as he heard to whose window the ladder led. 'Wait here,' he snapped to the anxious Bob. 'I'm going up to see what's happened.'

He began to mount the slender ladder swiftly. The lower sash of the window was open and the room was in complete darkness. But as his head rose level with the sill he became aware of a pungent smell that there was no mistaking.

Chloroform!

There was something very wrong here, he thought. The mystery had taken a new and even more sinister turn. Gripping the window frame, he flung one leg over the sill and pulled himself into the room. The spirituous smell of the drug was stronger. He went over to the door and pressed down the light switch.

The pendant light came on, and he saw that the room was empty! The bed was in a state of disorder and several articles of the girl's clothes lay scattered about. A patch of white on the floor near the bed attracted his attention, and he picked it up. It was a pad of cotton wool, still damp with the drug.

He went back to the window and called softly to Bob Alperton. 'Come up,' he said. 'Don't make a noise.'

Bob needed no second bidding. He was up the ladder in a matter of seconds and scrambling over the sill. 'What is it? What's happened?' he demanded. He looked swiftly round the room. 'Where's Kathleen?'

'She's been drugged and taken away somewhere,' said Heron. 'Smell the chloroform?'

'Good God! What can we do?' cried Bob.

'You can keep your voice down for a start,' said Heron. 'We don't want to rouse the house.'

'We must do something,' said Bob. 'We can't just stand here and — '

'Look here,' said Felix, 'we've no idea who's got her, or where they've taken her. What good can we do rushing about until

149

we know where we're going?'

'That's all very well,' argued Bob. 'But she may be in danger . . . Good Heavens, they may have killed her . . . '

'If they, whoever they are, had been going to kill her, they'd have done it here,' said Heron reasonably. 'Now, pull yourself together.' He went over to the door. It was locked and the key was not in the lock. 'That's queer. Why was the key taken?' he muttered.

'Shall I go for the police?' asked Alperton.

'Not yet.' Heron went over to the wardrobe and opened it. It was empty. 'I don't see any sign of the suit she was wearing when she came here,' he said. 'They must have taken her away in that.'

'Can't we do something?' exclaimed Bob irritably. 'What's the good of conjecturing? What does it matter what they took her away in? We want to find her before — '

'I know all that,' snapped Heron. 'I know how you feel, but it's no good going at this like a bull in a china shop.'

He began a swift search of the room

while the impatient Bob looked on, scarcely able to contain himself.

'There's nothing here. We'll go back down the ladder and see if there are any traces there.'

At the foot of the ladder there was a confused medley of footprints. Apart from his own and Alperton's, which were easy to distinguish, there were two others. But there was no sign of the girl's.

The appearance of the bed had perplexed him. It had been disturbed but it had, he was sure, never been slept in. There was no mark of a body having lain there, and the lower sheet was smooth and unwrinkled. The bed had been rumpled to give the impression that it had been slept in. But it hadn't. That meant that Kathleen Warrender had not gone to bed that night. But if she hadn't gone to bed, how had she been taken by surprise when the intruder had entered by the window? Why hadn't she given the alarm? There was a bell in every room.

Perhaps she had and no one had answered. Or had she rushed to the door to find it locked? If so, who had locked that door and removed the key? Someone in the house who was working in collusion with the unknown intruder?

Felix Heron considered all this while he followed the trail of the footprints which led away towards the drive. They were deeply indented, which seemed to suggest that the owners had been carrying a heavy weight. Kathleen, obviously. He followed them to the drive gates, and here he discovered the marks of tyres and a patch of oil. A car had stood there for some time.

Bob had followed him with growing annoyance. At last he burst out, 'Look here, I can't stand this fooling about any longer! I'm off to tell the police. The quicker they get things moving, the quicker we'll find Kathleen.'

'All right, off you go,' agreed Heron. 'Tell Hailsham, if you can find him, what's happened. Tell him the girl was taken away in a small car with Dunlop tyres, the front off-side cover having a crescent-shaped patch torn out.'

Bob was hurrying away when Heron called him back. 'Leave me the key. I can't get in without waking the house.'

Alperton pulled out the key and threw it over. 'See you back at the house,' he called, and vanished in the darkness.

For a little while after he had gone, Felix Heron continued his inspection of the roadway. There was nothing else. It was useless trying to trace the car, so he walked back quickly to the manor. Except for the light which he had left on in Kathleen's room, the place was in darkness. He admitted himself without noise, closed the door, and stood in the hall listening. There was no sound. The rest of the household had heard nothing, then, during the night.

Cautiously he mounted the staircase, and creeping along the corridor until he came to the girl's door, he looked at the lock. The key was there! The door had been locked from the outside! Someone in the house had locked that door.

Heron frowned. Surely the girl would have heard. Why hadn't she called out or made some kind of protest? It was very peculiar. Quite a considerable time must have elapsed after she had entered her room before the intruder had arrived. Or — wait! Had he been already there, waiting for her, with the drugged-soaked wadding ready to clap over her mouth? It didn't sound very likely. Anybody could have seen the ladder outside the window if it had been put there so early. It was a very puzzling problem.

The reason for the girl's abduction was not very difficult to understand. The person responsible was under the impression that she knew the whereabouts of the missing money, and was hoping to force her to speak. But the key proved that the unknown had a confederate in the house. Who was it?

Heron made his way quietly along to his own room. Carefully, so as not to wake Thelma, he opened the door and slipped into the room.

And then he got a shock. His wife was not there!

⋆   ⋆   ⋆

Thelma had spent a monotonous day. She had hoped that Felix would return

154

from London early and talk over what he had succeeded in unearthing. But he hadn't.

Harry had arrived shortly after the return of Gordon Lyle. And this was something. She could hear, at least, what Harry had been up to. But this proved to be very little. On reaching Waterloo, Lyle had hailed a taxi and been driven to the city. Here he had entered a block of offices in Slater Street, where he had remained for the best part of two hours. When he came out, he took another taxi to an exclusive restaurant in Piccadilly. Quite obviously his object was lunch. Harry was feeling hungry by this time but he dared not leave in case Lyle came out while he was away.

So he waited. And the wait was a long one. Lyle was not hurrying over his lunch. It was nearly three when he appeared again and walked slowly towards the Marble Arch. Turning down Park Lane, Lyle entered the vestibule of an expensive block of flats. This turned out to be the longest wait of all, for it was six o'clock before he came out, hailed a taxi and was driven to Waterloo. And that was all. Lyle had made no attempt to get away and there was nothing to show that he was mixed up in any way with the affair at Grandchester Manor.

Harry was tired, hungry, and rather fed up, and Thelma couldn't blame him. Benson supplied him with a meal, and he went to bed.

Thelma passed the rest of the evening as best she could. She talked to Kathleen while the others played their game of bridge. The girl was obviously as bored as Thelma, and very soon Thelma made an excuse and went up to her room.

But she couldn't sleep. She got a book and tried to read but her mind kept on wondering what Felix was doing. She heard the rest of the household going to their rooms, and later the sound of Benson making his rounds and locking up. Presently complete silence settled over the house as the occupants slept.

Thelma decided that she might as well do the same. She switched out the light over the bed and snuggled down into the pillow.

Suddenly she was wide awake and sitting up in bed. What was it that had disturbed her? Evidently she had fallen asleep. She could hear nothing. Yet something had wakened her.

And then she heard a gentle scraping noise. It came from somewhere outside in the darkness and was followed by the crunch of a footfall on gravel.

Thelma slipped out of bed and went over to the window. Cautiously she pulled back the curtains. She could see nothing. With infinite care she gently raised the sash of the window. It was raining heavily, and the cold drops pattered on her face as she leaned out.

The darkness was intense and it took her a little while before her eyes grew accustomed to it. Something was moving on the gravel path that encircled the house. Quite clearly now, she could hear the footsteps on the wet gravel.

The shadow moved again, and she saw that it was a man. She saw something else: the vague outline of a ladder that had been reared against the house. With a thrill, she saw the man start to ascend the ladder. The top scraped the brickwork as it bent slightly under the weight of the man who was mounting it.

Thelma withdrew her head quickly. She had brought a pair of slacks with her and these she found and pulled on over her pyjamas. A pullover completed her hasty toilet. Slipping an automatic into her pocket, she opened the door and tiptoed out into the passage.

The house was dark and silent. She made her way noiselessly to the head of the stairs. Only the ticking of the clock reached her ears as she paused to listen. She descended the stairs to the gloom of the hall.

She felt for the fastenings and discovered, to her surprise, that the front door was unchained and unbolted. She opened it cautiously a few inches and peered out.

Damp darkness; the sighing of the wind and the hiss of the falling rain. That was all. She opened the door wide enough to squeeze through, and pulled it shut so softly that it made no sound.

From the porch she could see nothing of the ladder or the man who had climbed it. She was wearing crêpe-soled shoes that made no noise as she went swiftly down the steps to the path and followed it round until she could see the ladder.

There was no sign of the man who had been there before; there was no sign of anything human.

Thelma watched, holding her breath. She felt that she was on the verge of an important discovery. And suddenly she heard a footstep *behind* her!

She hadn't expected anyone to come from this direction, but she slid behind a bush and strained her eyes to see who was approaching.

The figure of a man came out of the dark mouth of the drive. As he came nearer, she saw that it wasn't the same man who had climbed the ladder. This was a much bigger man. He wore a dripping raincoat and a cap that was pulled down over his eyes, so that she could make out nothing of his face. He hurried past her until he came to the foot of the ladder. Here, he stopped and tapped sharply on one of the wooden uprights.

There was an interval and something began to slide gently down the sloping ladder. It was a large bundle attached to a taut rope, and the man below stretched out his arms to receive it.

The man still holding the bundle, which Thelma could see from its shape was a human form, released the rope, jerked at it, and it was pulled up quickly. Carrying the body in his arms, the man began to return the way he had come. He passed close to where she crouched behind the bush and she saw that he was carrying the limp figure of Kathleen Warrender!

So that was it! They had abducted the girl!

Well, at any rate, thought Thelma, she would put a stop to that little plan! Her fingers closed over the butt of the automatic in her pocket, as she crept softly in the wake of the man with the girl.

He must have been quite strong for, in

spite of his burden, he never faltered and never looked back. Thelma kept to the grass edging of the drive, ready to slip into the bushes if he did.

He went on to the entrance gates, which were open, and he passed quickly through on to the road beyond. As she, too, came to the gates, Thelma saw a car standing, lightless, close by. The door was open and the unknown man was bundling Kathleen, who seemed quite unconscious, into the back when Thelma disclosed her presence.

'Who are you?' she demanded. 'What do you think you're doing?'

The man swung round with a startled oath. His face was covered by a dark scarf. Thelma saw his hand move toward his pocket.

'Put your hands up!' she ordered sharply. 'I've got a gun and I'll use it if you try anything!'

'Look here,' began the man.

'Take that scarf from your face,' broke in Thelma. 'I want to see what you look like.'

The other made no move to obey. His

hands remained quite still.

'Go on!' snapped Thelma. 'I'm getting cold and wet! Do as I tell you!' She made a movement with the automatic, and his hand went slowly up to his face. He was almost touching the concealing scarf when Thelma heard a sound — from behind her! She whirled quickly. But she was too late!

Something caught her a violent blow on the head, and the night exploded in a vivid flash of orange flame!

\* \* \*

The sky was grey with the coming dawn. The chill of early morning was in the damp air when Felix Heron, Hailsham, and Colonel Wickthorne gathered in the library at the manor to discuss the latest developments. Between them stood a tray of hot coffee, hastily spared by a sleepy-eyed and indignant servant roused from normal rest for this purpose. In front of the fireplace stood the dressing-gowned Sir Richard Alperton, pale and worried. On the arm of a chair, tired and wan, perched Bob Alperton.

'The description's gone out to all stations,' said Hailsham. 'Let's hope it does some good. What do you think has happened to your wife, sir?'

'I don't know,' said Felix. 'Something must have disturbed her during the night. She dressed in her slacks and a pullover, which are missing. Perhaps she saw something.'

'Regarding Miss Warrender?' asked Hailsham.

Felix nodded. 'I should think that was most likely.'

Bob jerked his head round. 'You think she saw what happened?'

'It's possible.'

'In that case, might she have followed these people?'

'If she has, we shall hear from her.'

'You don't seem very worried about her,' grunted Alperton.

'I gave up worrying about Thelma a long time ago,' said Heron. 'She can take care of herself and usually does.'

'What did they want with Kathleen?' went on Sir Richard, frowning.

'Well, that seems an easy one,' answered Felix. 'They think she's got the information they want.'

'Who the deuce can be at the bottom of this?' said Colonel Wickthorne irritably. He hadn't recovered from being dragged out of his bed in the middle of the night.

Nobody answered him because nobody knew.

'I suppose,' said Heron after a pause, 'when you took over this house, Alperton, you took over everything in it?'

'Yes, lock, stock, and barrel.'

Hailsham gave Heron a sharp glance. 'Are you suggesting, sir,' he said, 'that the money is concealed somewhere here?'

'Either here or at Cray's Lodge.'

'What's this about money?' asked Sir Richard.

Felix Heron explained, and Alperton pursed his lips. 'If you're right,' he said, 'I don't see how you're going to find it. Like looking for a needle in a haystack.'

'The person who's looking for it realises that,' answered Heron. 'That's why he's going to such trouble to discover the exact spot.'

'Seems a funny way to go about it,' put in Wickthorne. 'If, as you believe, Warrender knew, why kill him? Doesn't make sense. Killing the goose that might lay the golden egg, eh?'

'It's a puzzling point,' agreed Felix.

'It's not the only one,' grunted the colonel. 'It all puzzles me. And there's nothing to show that Bannister hid this money, if he ever had it, either here or at Cray's Lodge. He might have hidden it anywhere.'

'Look here,' said Bob, breaking a long silence. 'It's easy to believe that Warrender knew about it, and that Cassell may have known, too. They were both closely connected with Francis Bannister. But who else could know about it? Bannister isn't likely to have broadcast the fact that he was keeping back assets that should have gone to his creditors, is he? So how did this unknown chap get on to it?' He had put his finger on the most mysterious part of the whole business.

'Well, *somebody* knows. That's as far as we can go at the moment,' said Heron.

'We're going round and round in

circles, sir,' said Hailsham, 'and we're not getting anywhere.'

Felix was forced to agree. He was unaware how soon fresh evidence was to come into his possession. It came later that morning, after Wickthorne and Hailsham had gone to attend to the routine of the inquiries. And it came as the result of a chance remark made by Sir Richard Alperton as he and Felix strolled in the Tudor Garden before breakfast.

Heron was tired, and more worried about Thelma's absence than he cared to admit; and, in the hope that the fresh air would brighten him up, he had suggested a stroll.

'I doubt if I shall ever feel entirely happy here again,' remarked Alperton, after they had paced the length of the Tudor Garden in silence. 'It will always have these murders associated with it. Pity; I was getting very fond of the place.'

'It's a beautiful spot. One of the few fine houses left.'

'But you must understand how I feel? This garden — it's impossible to see it without remembering Cassell. I was planning a lot of alterations, too. Bannister's ideas didn't exactly coincide with mine. For instance, I bought the sundial and had it put in. What d'you think *he* hid there?'

'I've no idea.'

'A horrible leaden group — quite out of keeping with the setting. A sundial, of course, is just right. I was lucky to get one in the right period.' He swept his hand towards it. 'Can you imagine — a hideous group of three storks, not even very well executed.'

'Of course, the sundial is perfect,' began Heron. And then suddenly: 'What did you say? Did you say something about storks?'

'It's not important.'

'But it is — it's very important.'

Sir Richard looked at him kindly. 'Why not have a lie down for a bit?' he suggested.

'Look here, tell me about those storks.'

'Well, I've told you. There was a horrible group of leaden storks — '

'What happened to it?' A faint flush had come into Heron's cheeks. He

167

remembered the scrap of paper that Thelma had found in the study at Cray's Lodge: ' ... ird St ... ' Could the completed message read, 'Third Stork'?

'I told the gardener to get rid of the things.'

'Were they separate?'

'Yes. They were stuck in a slab of concrete. You've never seen anything so —'

'Where is the gardener?' broke in Heron. 'Is he here?'

'I expect he's around somewhere. Look here, what the deuce is the matter with you?' Sir Richard stared his astonishment.

'It's all right,' answered Heron. 'Let's find the gardener, if we can.'

The bewildered, and a little annoyed, Sir Richard shrugged his shoulders. 'I can't see what you're so excited about,' he grumbled.

'I'll explain later,' promised Heron. 'I assure you, it's very important that we find the gardener.'

'We'll go and look for him, if you insist,' said Alperton resignedly. 'Come along.'

They found the gardener working on one of the mixed borders. He was an ancient man whose brain worked slowly. 'Them there storks?' he said. 'Yes. Made of lead they was. Sir Richard wanted me to get rid of 'em.'

'What did you do with them?'

The old man appeared to take this as a slur upon his honesty. 'They was give ter me,' he protested. 'That's right, sir, ain't it?' he appealed to Alperton.

'That's right, Eales.'

'Ah!' The gardener looked at Heron triumphantly. 'There, yer. I didn't do nuthin' wrong.' He wiped his hand across his nose. 'I ain't got 'em.'

'What did you do with them?' asked Heron.

'Sold 'em ter Joe Pigeon, wot keeps the nursery garden in the village,' answered Eales. He rubbed his bristling chin with a gnarled knuckle.

'How long ago was this?'

The gardener screwed up his eyes in an effort of memory. 'Let me see now. It'd be just afore I put in them bulbs . . . ah yes, that's when it'd be.'

'When was that?'

Eales was not to be hurried. This is a peculiarity of professional gardeners; nothing on earth will induce them to hurry.

'Now, how long would it be? About four months . . . yes that'd be about it . . . four months.'

'Thank you, Eales,' said Felix. 'That's all I wanted to know. Come on, Alperton. I'm going to see Pigeon.'

The puzzled gardener stared after them curiously. Then he spat thoughtfully and continued his job.

The owner of the nursery garden in the village was a lean, dried-up little man who listened in silence to what Heron had to say.

'Yes, sir, I bought them storks from Eales,' he said. 'I've still got one of 'em.'

'Can I see it?' asked Heron quickly.

For an answer, Mr. Pigeon led the way to a small building used as a shop and office. The counter was piled with all kinds of garden requisites.

'There you are, sir,' said Mr. Pigeon. 'I took 'em off the concrete. They looked better separate.'

Felix Heron went over and inspected the leaden figure. It was very badly cast and stood about a yard high, one of the long legs drawn up.

'Were the others exactly like this one?' he asked.

'No, sir, they was all different. One 'ad a fish in its mouth, an' the other was sort of leaning down with its neck stretched out.'

'What happened to these other two?'

'I sold 'em,' said Mr. Pigeon. 'There's some what likes that sort o' thing to stick round a pond. I got 'em cheap an' sold 'em cheap — two quid apiece.'

'Who did you sell them to?'

But Mr. Pigeon had exhausted his information. 'They was just casual customers. They took 'em away with 'em.'

'I'd like to have known who bought them,' said Heron. 'Never mind. I'll take this one.' He extracted two one-pound notes from his wallet and handed them to the nursery-man. 'You needn't trouble to wrap it up,' he said. 'I'll take it as it is.' He tucked the stork under his arm and went back to the car, followed by the astonished Alperton.

'Are you quite mad?' he demanded. 'What did you want to buy that damned thing for?'

'I think it has a very distinct bearing on the murders.'

'I suppose you know what you're doing,' grunted Sir Richard.

'I hope so,' replied Heron.

He wasn't yet prepared to go into a detailed explanation. He wanted to be more certain that he was right before committing himself. And when they reached the manor a surprise awaited them that put everything else out of his mind for the time being.

Benson was at the front door, and he came forward to meet them as they got out of the car,

'Miss Warrender's come back, sir,' he announced.

# 11

Kathleen Warrender opened her eyes, and
her first sensation was feeling sick. The
next was a sense of movement. Her
mouth was dry, and there was a tightness
at her temples, as though something had
been bound round her head. She became
aware of a continuous swishing noise,
accompanied by a rhythmic throbbing.
There was a light somewhere that danced
about spasmodically, and quite suddenly
she realised that she was in a car that was
moving at a considerable speed.

In a hazy state of semi-consciousness,
she puzzled over this. She remembered
going to bed, or rather, she remembered
going to her room. After that she couldn't
remember very much. What had happened?

She had drunk the glass of water which
was her nightly habit, and then — a total
blank! She could recollect nothing until
now, when she found herself sitting in a

car that was speeding through darkness. The mists were clearing rapidly however, and she could make out a dim figure beside her; a bulky figure clad in a heavy coat, whose gloved hands rested on the wheel. She moved uneasily and moaned. The figure turned its head.

'Recovering?' asked a gruff voice. 'Take it easy and you'll be all right.'

Her throat was so dry that at first she could not speak. At the third attempt she managed to utter three words: 'Where am I?'

'There's nothing to be afraid of,' said the gruff voice. 'You'll not be hurt. If I were you, I'd keep quiet for a bit longer.'

Kathleen decided that this must be a particularly vivid dream. It couldn't be real. She closed her eyes and floated away on a sea of unconsciousness again.

When she came to herself the swishing and the throbbing had stopped. There was no longer any sense of motion. The figure beside her still sat there, but his hands no longer rested on the wheel.

Her mind was suddenly quite clear and she tried to struggle up with a frightened cry. A firm hand caught her arm.

'Keep still!' ordered the voice that had spoken before. 'There's no need to get scared.'

But she was scared. She stared fearfully at the figure beside her but she could see nothing, only a shadowy bulk. The car had stopped somewhere in the open country. She knew this because of the sound of the wind in the trees, but she could see nothing, for the car's lights had been turned out.

'Why have I been brought here?' she demanded huskily.

'I want to have a little talk with you,' answered the man at the wheel. 'Feeling all right now?'

'Who are you?' she asked.

'That doesn't matter,' said the man, and as she turned toward him: 'You won't find out that way.'

She realised the truth of this. A scarf covered his face so that only his eyes were visible beneath the cap he wore.

'You've nothing to be afraid of,' the voice went on. 'No harm will come to you. I only wish to talk to you.'

She moistened her dry lips with the tip of her tongue. 'What about?' she asked.

'I'll tell you,' he answered. 'I want to know what's happened to the group of three storks that used to be in the Tudor Garden at Grandchester Manor.'

She stared at him blankly. 'I don't know what you mean.'

'You've never seen them?'

She shook her head.

'They were there when Francis Bannister lived there. Where are they now? What has happened to them?'

'I can't tell you,' she answered. 'If you thought I could, you've had your trouble for nothing.'

'You're sure? You're telling the truth?'

'I know nothing about them,' she asserted.

'Think!' he urged. 'Didn't your father ever mention them?'

'Father? No, why should he?'

'Warrender must have been the person who moved them,' muttered the man. 'He must have . . .'

A conviction suddenly came to her, and she shrank away from him.

'It was you,' she accused. 'It was you who killed my father.'

'Why should you think that?' he demanded harshly.

'I'm sure it was. You shot him and you searched the house. You were looking for those things — the storks.'

'You seem to know a lot,' he said. 'Supposing I admit that it was me — what then?'

'What are you going to do with me?'

'I've told you already that you are in no danger,' he snapped. 'I hoped you could give me some information. Since you can't, you no longer interest me!'

He moved abruptly, and she almost screamed. But he only switched on the lights. The beam from the car's lights lit up a green tunnel and she guessed that they had stopped in a narrow lane.

'You are certain that you know nothing of the whereabouts of that group?' he demanded.

'Nothing. I know nothing.'

His eyes above the scarf searched her face steadily. 'I believe you,' he said abruptly, and pressed his foot on the starter. The engine sprang to life almost instantly, and the car moved forward.

'Where are you taking me?' she asked nervously.

'You'll see.'

Slowly the car nosed its way to the end of the lane. They turned into a wider road, and the speed increased. For what seemed an age the car sped through the darkness, and then suddenly he brought it to a stop. 'Get out!' he ordered.

'What do you mean?' she demanded.

'Get out!' he repeated curtly. 'I am leaving you here. You can find your way back.'

'But where am I?' she asked in dismay.

'You must find out for yourself!' he retorted. 'Go on, hurry up. I want to get on.'

She opened the door and stepped out into the wet roadway. Instantly the car door was slammed and it shot forward with a jerk, spattering her with mud from the wheels. The red tail-light vanished in the distance, and with a shiver she looked about her. The road was quite unfamiliar to her. Thick woods behind stretched away on either side. She had no knowledge of where she was. She could be within a few minutes' walk of Grandchester Manor, or miles away.

The night was cold and she shivered violently. It was no good standing still. She began to walk slowly in the direction from whence the car had come, but her progress was slow. Her knees shook and she felt weak and ill. The drug was still active in her system and she experienced a return of the faintness. She felt dizzy and she staggered slightly. The roadway and the dark, gaunt trees that lined it danced jerkily before her eyes.

She passed her hand across her eyes, but the dizziness persisted. There was a dark heap at the side of the road, and she discovered that it was a pile of stones left there by some road menders. She sank down on the heap gratefully, her aching legs giving way under her. Her head was throbbing, and although she was shivering she felt hot and feverish.

After a few minutes she tried to get up. Everything whirled round her, she slipped forward and for the third time that night lost consciousness . . .

It was daylight when she came back to her senses. In the quiet, still grey of early morning, she was stiff with cold and her hands felt numb. She rubbed them vigorously and then massaged her legs to get some life into them. The throbbing in her head, however, had stopped. She still felt weak and shaky, but when she struggled to her feet she found that she could stand.

She tried to decide which direction she should take. Since she had no idea which led where, it didn't seem to matter. She decided to continue in the same direction she had been going when the faintness overtook her. Desperately cold and more miserable than she had ever been before in her life, she trudged along, hoping that she might meet someone who could tell her where she was. But she met no one and the rough road seemed endless. It got narrower, merging at last into what was little more than a footpath.

She followed this, twisting through the woodland, and was forced to the unpleasant conclusion that she was completely lost. She sat down on a fallen tree-trunk to rest. Perhaps she ought to have gone the other way. Perhaps she had just been increasing the distance between herself and the manor. But she didn't feel strong enough to retrace her steps. It would be better to go on and hope that she would find somebody who could tell her the right way.

She forced herself to get up and continue. After while the woods began to thin and she came to a main road. There was something familiar about it, and then she recognised it. It was the road that ran through the village. With renewed energy and hope she hurried on. It wouldn't be long now, but it seemed an eternity. When she finally staggered up the drive to the manor she was almost exhausted.

She just had sufficient strength to ring the bell, and then she collapsed on the steps, where Benson found her when he came to open the front door in answer to her ring.

'Pity you can't identify the man in the car,' said Felix Heron. He was sitting on the side of the girl's bed, where she had been carried at once by Agatha Hughes.

'I never saw his face,' she said.

'What about his voice?'

'It was low and gruff. I don't think it was his real voice.'

Her eyes were tired, and there were dark circles under them which showed up against the dead whiteness of her face.

Heron had only been allowed to see her for a few minutes. Agatha Hughes wanted her to get a good sleep and a long one. But he had hoped that she might have some vital information. It was a disappointment that she could tell him nothing.

'It seems rather a senseless thing to risk abducting you, only to let you go again,' he said, frowning.

'Oh, didn't I tell you? He asked me about some storks.'

Heron uttered an exclamation. 'Tell me exactly what he said.'

She did so. 'He seemed to think that I ought to know about the things,' she ended. 'He hinted that my father might have mentioned them to me. I don't know what he was talking about.'

'I do,' said Heron. That accidental remark of Sir Richard's had been of more importance than he'd thought. And here was confirmation. Francis Bannister had hidden the two hundred thousand that he had stolen from his creditors in one of those leaden figures. The third one, according to the scrap of paper. And someone who knew was making frantic efforts to find it. The motive was clear. But who was the man in the car? That was still a mystery.

'Your father never mentioned these things?'

'No. What are they? Why was this man so anxious to find them?'

'It's too long to tell you now,' said Heron. He got up. 'The best thing for you is lots of sleep.'

He went down the stairs to the library, where he found Alperton waiting impatiently. 'Well, could she tell you anything helpful?' asked the latter.

'Quite a lot,' answered Felix.

'Who took her away?'

'I don't know, but I know why. He thought she might know what had happened to the storks.'

Sir Richard stared at him as if he'd gone mad. 'Stop talking in riddles and do a little explaining,' he growled. 'What is the interest in those damned things?'

'Come along to the garage,' answered Felix.

Muttering below his breath, Alperton followed him. Heron was carrying the stork which he had left on a chair in the library when Benson had told them of the return of Kathleen Warrender. When they reached the garage Heron found a hacksaw, and putting the lead figure on a bench, he carefully started to cut off the neck close to where it joined the body. It was not difficult. The stork was hollow. In a few minutes, he was able to see inside the hollow interior.

'Not this one,' he muttered. 'Quite empty.'

'What the devil did you expect to find?' demanded Sir Richard.

'I hoped to find two hundred thousand pounds, or its equivalent,' replied Felix.

Into Alperton's puzzled eyes came a look of understanding. 'Bannister's money? But why in there?'

'It's in one of those storks,' said Heron.

'How do you know?'

Felix was going to explain when Thelma came into the garage. Her face was white, and her hair a tangled mass. Her slacks and pullover were stained, wet, and muddy. She was breathing quickly.

'Hello,' said Felix. 'Where did you spring from? I've been worried about you.'

'I've been up in the wood near Cray's Lodge for most of the night,' she said.

'You look a mess,' remarked Heron, eyeing her critically.

'So would you, if you'd been tied up half the night in that foul wood!' she retorted. 'I suppose you know that Kathleen Warrender was abducted last night?'

'She's come back,' said Heron.

Thelma put up her hand and pushed the hair out of her eyes. 'Come back, has she? What happened? Did she get away from that man in the car?'

Felix told her. 'Now tell me what happened to you,' he finished.

Briefly she told him about her adventure of the night. 'When I came to my senses I found that I'd been tied up and put in the undergrowth in that wood that stretches from the back of Cray's Lodge. I was soaked through and cold as an iceberg. It took me ages to get free, and I called and called but nobody answered. As soon as I was free I hurried here. That's all.'

'Let me see where the other man hit you,' said Heron. She pushed back her hair. There was a bruise on the side of her head but the skin was unbroken.

'A sandbag, I should think,' remarked Felix. 'Did you see anything of this other man?'

'Not a thing. I didn't expect anyone to creep up behind me. But I can tell you one thing — this man in the car has an accomplice in the house.'

'That's impossible!' broke in Sir Richard.

'It's true, all the same,' said Heron. 'The glass of water that Kathleen Warrender drank was doped. That was done from inside, and so was the locking of her door.'

186

'Who could it be?' demanded Alperton.

Heron shrugged his shoulders. 'I don't know. What we've got to do now is find who bought those other two storks.'

'What storks?' asked his wife.

'Oh, you don't know, do you?' he said.

'How could I? Perhaps you've forgotten that I've been lying in some filthy undergrowth in a stinking wood all night!'

'And you should go and have a hot bath, a good stiff Johnnie Walker, and go to bed,' said Heron.

'You just tell me about these storks,' she said, 'and then I'll think about it.'

Felix knew that the only way to get her to do what he wanted was to tell her, so he did so. 'Pigeon sold the other two, but he doesn't know the people who bought 'em,' he concluded. 'We've got to find them before our unknown friend does.'

'You've got a difficult job,' grunted Alperton. 'Pigeon's nurseries are known all over the district. Hundreds of people buy their garden stuff there. Some of them come from miles away. How the deuce are you going to trace two people out of — '

'Hailsham,' interrupted Heron. 'He can do that. His organisation will cover the ground quicker than we can.'

'Look,' said Thelma, 'that money must have been converted into something less bulky. You couldn't get two hundred thousand pounds in that thing.' She pointed to the decapitated stork on the bench.

'Diamonds, or something equally valuable,' said Heron. 'Now, off you go to bed.'

Thelma went. She was longing for hot water to take the chill from her bones, followed by the soft comfort of her bed. And the soothing effect of a hot mixture of Johnnie Walker.

'Who can be behind this business?' asked Alperton when she had gone.

'I wish I knew,' answered Felix. 'I'd like to know why your telephone was put out of action on the night Cassell was killed. There doesn't seem any reason for that.'

'To delay the alarm being given.'

Heron shook his head. 'That wouldn't be it. There's some other reason.' He yawned and stretched himself. 'I think I'll have a hot bath and change. Then I'll go and see Hailsham.'

'I could do with a drink,' said Alperton. 'Come into the library. I'm sure you could do with a Johnnie Walker, too.'

A little later, on his way to the bathroom, Heron passed Benson in the hall. A thought occurred to him and he stopped. 'Have you been employed here long, Benson?' he asked.

'About five months, sir.'

'Where were you employed before?'

'I was valet to an American gentleman, sir.'

'You don't know this district very well?

The butler shook his head. 'Not very well, sir.'

Heron went on up the stairs. Luxuriating in a hot bath, he thought over all that he knew of this strange business. And suddenly an idea came to him.

It was startling, and at first seemed too fantastic to be given credence.

But the more he thought about it, the more certain he became that it was the right solution.

# 12

The almost impossible idea which had flashed into Felix Heron's mind in his bath continued to fill it while he dressed. It was only a theory without the smallest piece of concrete evidence to back it up, but it fit all the known facts. It explained the unexplainable. It accounted for everything that had happened in this strangest of cases.

He decided, for the moment, to keep his idea to himself. It might turn out to be quite impossible when it came to the test.

When he was dressed — he had used another room put at his disposal by Sir Richard to avoid disturbing Thelma — he peeped into the other bedroom to see how his wife was. She was fast asleep and he went quietly out again, closing the door. It would do her good. Both she and Kathleen needed all the rest they could get after their adventures of the night.

Heron sought out Harry. 'I'm going up to London,' said the former. 'There's a little job I'd like you to do with Superintendent Hailsham while I'm away.'

'When are you going?' asked Harry.

'Now!' answered Heron.

'I'll get the car round,' said Harry, and departed.

'I'm calling at the police station first,' said Felix a few minutes later as they sped down the drive. 'I'll explain what I want you to do.' He told Harry about the storks. 'We've got to find out who bought those other two. But it must be done quietly. This man who's after them mustn't get to hear until we're ready.'

'I see,' said Harry. 'You're going to use the right one for a trap?'

There were no flies on Harry. He went straight to the essential point, like a homing pigeon. It was uncanny sometimes how he could almost follow your unspoken thoughts.

'That's the idea,' agreed Heron. 'He'll come after the spoils and we'll catch him.'

They found Hailsham in the tiny office

at the back of the charge-room. He was looking despondent and very tired. 'There's no news of the girl,' he began when Felix came in.

'Don't worry, she's back,' said Heron. He explained what had happened, and before the surprised superintendent had time to comment, went on, 'We've got to find the people who bought those other storks. The money's in one of them. We can be sure of that after what this man said to Miss Warrender.'

'I agree,' said Hailsham.

'I'm going up to London. I've got an inquiry to make. So I'm leaving you and my secretary to get on with the search.'

Hailsham scratched the side of his chin. 'It's not going to be easy,' he grunted.

'I know, but it's important. Do your best. Harry will do everything he can to help. If we can find those storks we'll have our murderer trapped in no time.'

'I'll do my best,' said Hailsham. 'I'll try an' get some men drafted from Oxford.'

'Don't make a song and dance about it,' warned Felix. 'If the man we're after gets to hear where these things are before

I do, we can say goodbye to him and the money.' He left Hailsham and went out to his car, followed by Harry.

'Now,' said Felix as he climbed into his car, 'I shall be back late tonight. If you get any news, phone the flat and tell Thelma, will you, that I've gone to London to follow up an inquiry.'

He pressed on the starter and the powerful engine hummed to life. Waving his hand to his secretary, he sped away down the road and vanished round the bend.

\* \* \*

Chief Superintendent Manning looked up from a littered desk as Heron was shown into his cheerless office at Scotland Yard. 'Hello, Heron,' he greeted. 'Glad to see you. Take a pew. Look at all this stuff!' He pointed disgustedly to the desk. 'Reports an' forms in triplicate! How can they expect you to catch crooks when it's a full-time job filling in and signing these damned things? So far as I can make out, nobody reads 'em.'

Felix was sympathetic. He knew that the paperwork which each senior member of the police force had to deal with had increased out of all reason in the last few years. 'I won't keep you long,' he said. 'I just want a spot of information.'

'You're always welcome to anything I can do,' said Manning. He looked at his watch. 'I've got to see the A.C. in half an hour. Will that do?'

'Should be ample,' said Heron. 'Listen, I'll tell you what I want.' Without waste of words, he told him.

Manning's eyebrows rose as he listened. 'What's the idea?' he said.

'I'll tell you that after you've given me the information I want,' said Heron.

'Same old story. Close as an oyster,' grunted Manning. He picked up the house telephone and gave an extension number. 'Hello, Charley? Manning here. Listen ... ' He explained what he required. 'Send it down, will you? Thanks.' He slammed the receiver back on its rack.

'I was going to suggest that you came out to lunch with me,' said Heron.

'I'll be lucky if I get a beer and a sandwich,' said Manning. 'Thanks all the same. I'd've liked to. No wonder there's a crime wave! All these damned regulations! And when you do catch 'em, what happens these days? They almost give 'em a medal! Abolish this, abolish that! I'd like to abolish some of these stupid politicians and cranks who don't know what they're talking about! If they got about more among the people they want to reform by kid glove methods they'd know all about it! Committees! Bah!'

Heron agreed with him. Manning had risen from the ranks and he knew what he was talking about. There was only one deterrent, and that was swift and severe punishment. There was a new type of criminal bred from the hooligans who had been allowed to multiply while futile theorists talked poppycock about 'mixed-up kids' and similar claptrap. The only things these inhuman beasts understood was fear. They ruled by fear! And authority expected to put a stop to their activities by giving them more playing fields! More youth clubs! It wasn't because they were bored that they descended in hordes on seaside towns and smashed everything that came in their way. This was their idea of enjoyment. This was the result of the present method of education that spent millions on teaching them the three 'R's but never taught them how to behave, or instilled in their minds any standards to live up to, except as a vague sideline. Or taught them how to speak the Queen's English.

And these worthless parasites bred fast, fostered by the present laxity of the very people who should know better. Unless really drastic methods were used to stamp them out, as they should have been at the very beginning, these louts would increase in numbers until they became a very real danger to the community. But the powers that be, like ostriches, stuck their thick heads in the sands of complacency and pretended that the danger was not there. One day, they might wake up — when it was too late.

A messenger came in and laid a file on Manning's desk. 'Here you are. Here's the full report,' said Manning.

Felix Heron pulled up his chair, and together they skimmed through the typewritten sheets. There was a gleam in Heron's eyes when they had finished. 'I believe I'm right,' he said.

Manning gave a grunt. 'Probably,' he said. 'You usually are. What are you right about?'

Heron leaned forward. He spoke rapidly and at almost his first words, Manning's face changed. With his expression passing from astonishment to incredulity, he listened without comment.

'It's impossible!' he declared when Heron finished.

'Incredible, but not impossible. Of course, it's still got to be proved.'

'That's going to be difficult. You've got to account for this other man. Who was he?'

'That's where I want your help,' said Felix.

'I'll do all I can, because I think you're right. But you've got to prove it. Without any shadow of doubt. It accounts for everything . . . '

'Except the cutting of those telephone wires.'

The other made a gesture. 'Is that very important?' he asked.

'I think so. There's no reason why they should have been. Everything else fits, but that doesn't.' He took out a cigarette, gave one to Manning, and lit them both. 'The main thing, of course, is to prove that my theory is fact.'

They discussed the matter until it was time for the chief superintendent to keep his appointment with the A.C., and Manning jotted down several notes.

Felix Heron arrived at Park Lane to the surprise of Miss Climp later that afternoon, having had lunch at his club. Going into his bedroom, he lay down for a rest before driving back to the manor.

There was still a lot to do, but the main puzzle was clear. He fell asleep, contented that it would not be long before he had the murderer under lock and key.

★   ★   ★

198

When he had served dinner that evening, Benson's duties were over for the day. He had asked for, and been given, permission to go out, and when the meal had been cleared away he went up to his room and changed his clothes. He looked thoughtful as he dressed, and his thoughts, to judge from his face, were not entirely pleasant.

The truth was that Benson was just a little uneasy. The events of the last few days had worried him. The close proximity of so many members of the police force was not at all to his liking.

There were certain documents in C.R.O. at New Scotland Yard which gave a detailed, and not very attractive, biography of Benson, though they were not filed under that name. This was immaterial, since the butler during his life had passed under many names, the most familiar one to the police being the one under which he had received his three convictions. It was not really, therefore, surprising that he should feel worried at the constant coming and going to the house of his natural enemies.

He wasn't very disturbed at the presence of Felix Heron. He looked upon him as an amateur, and not very dangerous. He had no reason to suppose that he was under any suspicion, and with that supreme vanity that marks the habitual criminal, he was sure that he had carried off his role of butler completely successfully. No one was likely to suspect that Benson the butler was Tommy Leftwich, the man who under numerous aliases had succeeded in getting away with more portable property in the shape of money and jewellery than most people in his profession. For the quiet-faced Benson was a crook, and if his methods lacked originality they were certainly successful, up to a point.

He had always worked along similar lines, for another characteristic of the professional criminal is that he fights shy of anything new. The confidence man sticks to one story; the burglar who uses a pantry window to gain admittance will always use that window, and disdain any other. Scotland Yard has a very complete index of what are known as 'modus operandi' cards, which set forth in detail all these peculiarities of the criminals who come under their survey. More crooks have been caught by their 'methods' than in any other way. A man who takes a drink of tea on the scene of his crime will always make himself tea. And any other habitual action. It is a constant wonder to the men whose duty it is to catch them that they are so blind as not to realise this. But they don't. And in most cases they might just as well sign their name to the job.

And Mr. Leftwich was no exception to the rule. His method had always been to secure a job as butler or valet in some rich household, and at his leisure to make off with such items of jewellery and other valuables as he could lay his hands on. Armed with a number of forged references, obtained easily by someone in 'the trade' from a gentleman in the East End of London, who made a speciality of such things, and quite a considerable profit, he experienced no difficulty in obtaining the desired situation. The present shortage of all domestic staff was a great help. People were only too willing to get hold of any kind of servant, even without bothering too much about references, but Mr. Leftwich always produced the highest. When he had told Felix Heron that he had been valet to an American gentleman, he had stated no more than the truth. He had omitted to mention that his employer had awakened one morning to find both his valet and his personal jewellery gone, together with three hundred and sixty odd pounds that he had taken from his bank on the previous afternoon. His reason for securing the job with Sir Richard Alperton had been similar, and it was pure accident that had shown him a safer and more profitable line of business.

The cut telephone wires which had puzzled Felix Heron were no mystery to Mr. Leftwich, for he had taken particular pains to cut them himself in order that his departure with certain valuables should not be prematurely reported to the police. He invariably took this precaution, for even half an hour's grace in a getaway was worth the trouble, as he had experienced.

But his accidental witnessing of Cassell's murder had altered all his ideas.

He had packed up several items that would fetch a good price from old Steinman, and was preparing to slip away with them when he had almost run into Norman Cassell, in dressing gown and slippers. He had effaced himself quickly behind a curtain and watched Cassell let himself quietly out. Mr. Leftwich was a curious man. He followed Cassell and saw the crime committed that was to cause such a sensation on the following morning.

It also provided him with a far better way of getting money than the few paltry trifles he was taking to Steinman. He was one of the few professional crooks who always carried a gun. He was thankful that night for the habit, for with the small automatic he had held up the man who had stabbed Cassell, and in the privacy of the Tudor Garden a bargain had been struck — a bargain that had sent Mr. Leftwich hurrying back to replace all the articles he had packed to take away.

A very large sum was within his grasp.

He had been promised ten thousand pounds for his silence and his help: an enormous sum to Mr. Leftwich, and very pleasant to look forward to.

His mind was full of this as he changed into the tweed suit which he wore on the occasions when he was off duty. With ten thousand pounds he could leave the country and spend a couple of years in a more congenial and warmer climate.

He whistled softly through his thin lips as he pictured what a wonderful time he was going to have. And there was no danger of his partner double-crossing him. Mr. Leftwich was far too wily to leave such a possible loophole. He fully realised that he was dealing with a dangerous man, and had taken a very necessary precaution. He had deposited with his bank a sealed envelope to be opened on his death, and that envelope contained all that he knew of the murder of Cassell. He had been glad that he had taken this precaution when he had seen the expression on the other's face when he had told him.

He put on his coat, and leaving the

house by the back entrance, set off in the direction of the village. At a small public house at the foot of the High Street he stopped to fortify himself with a large Johnnie Walker before proceeding to the serious business of the evening. There was plenty of time. His appointment was not for another hour. Leisurely, he consumed two more Johnnie Walkers, chatting to the girl behind the bar.

A pleasantly warm glow suffused him when he finally left and turned in the direction of a secondary thoroughfare that intersected the main road half a mile further on. Walking along this, he presently halted a few yards away from a milestone. Lighting a cigarette, he halted by the stone to await the arrival of his partner.

The time of the appointment was for ten, and it was two minutes to the hour when he saw the dim lights of a car approaching. It came rapidly nearer and stopped opposite him.

Mr. Leftwich crossed quickly, opened the door, and squeezed into the seat beside the driver. He pulled the door shut and the car moved off.

'What happened to the girl? Did she get back all right?' said the man in the driving seat.

'Yes. I let her in myself. Pretty well done in, she was.'

'And the other one?'

'Mrs. Nosy Heron? Yes, she got back, too.'

'Well, it was a lot of trouble for nothing,' grunted the man. 'We didn't get what we wanted.'

'No, but I have,' said Mr. Leftwich. 'I know what happened to those storks.'

The driver turned so quickly that the car swerved.

'Here — easy!' cried Mr. Leftwich in alarm.

'Tell me — where are they? Quick, where?'

'Sir Richard had 'em removed and gave 'em to the gardener. He sold 'em to a chap named Pigeon.'

'And I was sure Warrender had them. We must get them from this man Pigeon at once.'

'You can't,' interrupted Mr. Leftwich.

'He's sold 'em. He sold one to Heron. The other two have gone to two unknown people.'

The man behind the wheel uttered an oath. 'Heron! Why the hell did he want it? He can't know.'

'That's the point — he does,' said Mr. Leftwich. 'I heard him tell Alperton. I was listening outside the library door. He's found out about the figures an' he knows what's in one of 'em. Lucky it wasn't in the one he got hold of.'

'If he knows, he'll be after the other two.'

'He is,' snapped Mr. Leftwich curtly.

The driver slowed the car to a snail's pace. 'We've got to beat him to it,' he said. 'We must find them before he does.'

'Why? Why not let him find 'em?'

'Are you mad?'

'No, I'm being practical. We can't make inquiries, can we? So how can we find the things? Let Heron an' the police do the work. When they find 'em, we'll step in an' collect the loot.'

His suggestion was received in silence at first. Then: 'You're right!' exclaimed the driver after a long pause. 'But how are we going to keep a check on them? We've got to know the moment they know. Otherwise, it'll be too late.'

'Leave that to me. I'm just as interested as you. I want my ten thousand quid.'

'If anything goes wrong . . . '

'It won't. I'll guarantee we get our hands on 'em in time. Don't you worry!'

'I suppose your scheme's the only way.'

'You bet it is,' said Mr. Leftwich. 'Take me back and drop me near the manor. I've had a heavy day, an' what with that an' being up half the night over that girl, I can do with some sleep!'

# 13

Felix Heron did not get back to Grandchester Manor until eleven o'clock on the following morning. He was met by Harry with a gloomy face.

'Nothing doing up to now,' said the secretary. 'I just come in for a break. Superintendent Hailsham's got six men on the job. Result — nix!'

'Did you get a description of the purchasers from Pigeon?' asked Heron.

'We tried, but his description was so vague it would have fit half the people in the district. We're using the traveller stunt at the moment. Practically making a house-to-house search. Takes time, that's the trouble.'

'Got them travelling in garden produce?' asked Heron.

Harry nodded.

'Whose idea was that?'

'Well, it was mine.'

'It's a jolly good one,' declared Felix.

'Full marks, Harry!'

Harry was pleased. He smiled, which consisted of a slight twitching of the corners of his mouth, the nearest he ever got. 'It seems to be working,' he said. 'They're supposed to be specialising in garden ornaments. When they strike a house that's already got some, they ask if they might look at them in case they were made by the firm they are representing. They want to check up on the popularity of their products. You'd never credit the things they've seen! Toadstools, an' frogs, an' gnomes — everything but storks.'

'Well we can't hurry matters,' said Heron. 'I've plenty to do regarding another part of this business.'

He went off to find Thelma, and discovered her in the drawing room by herself.

'Well, well,' she remarked. 'So you've got back. What happened?'

Felix was vague. He hadn't told her of the idea that had come to him in his bath on the previous day, and he had no intention of doing so until it was more certain. Thelma, who knew this vague and reticent mood of old, knew that it was a good sign. While Felix was searching for a solution, he was ready enough to discuss the matter from all angles. It was only when he had formed an opinion and was waiting for proof that he became so exasperatingly uncommunicative. This habit had driven Thelma nearly mad when she had first known him, but she had got used to it by now and could treat it fairly calmly. There was no other way.

There was in Felix Heron a latent streak of the dramatic which insisted that he should present the denouement as a surprise and at exactly the right moment. It was the instinct of the artist, and Felix revelled in these last minute revelations. It was his moment. He looked forward to it with the eager anticipation that a playwright awaits his first night.

While this final stage was in process of fruition he was apt to become a little irritable; the more delay in acquiring the final items he required, the more irritable he became. And so it was with this present case. For two days there was a period of complete blank. Doggedly, Hailsham's men went from door to door, and discovered nothing. No sign of a leaden stork anywhere.

During this period of waiting there arrived in the village a shabbily dressed stranger who unobtrusively booked a room at the inn, informing the landlord that he was a student of botany. His studies were, for such a self-confessed enthusiast, peculiar to say the least, for he appeared to take a greater interest in Grandchester Manor and its inhabitants than in the flora and fauna of the district. If Felix Heron noticed the presence of this individual he gave no sign, and certainly no one else was aware of the newcomer who took every precaution to avoid making himself conspicuous.

On the morning of the third day, Felix received a telephone call from Chief Superintendent Manning — the cut wires had been restored — and, after a hurried word with Thelma, left for London. He spent a couple of hours with Manning and returned in the highest of good spirits, and with a sparkle in his eyes that warned Thelma that a crisis was near at hand.

'Very shortly now, dear,' he replied in answer to her question, 'we shall be able to put a name to the murderer!'

'Do you know who it is?' she asked.

He nodded. 'I've guessed for some time. I want two further items of information, and then I shall know for certain.' And with that, for the time being, she had to be content.

But the two items he was waiting for took a long time to turn up. The fourth and the fifth day came and went, and then on the sixth a telephone message from Hailsham sent Felix post-haste to the police station.

'I think we've found one of those storks, sir,' said the superintendent. 'There's a chap over at Streatley who bought it from Pigeon about a couple o' months ago.'

'Fine!' answered Felix. 'What's his name?'

Hailsham consulted a slip of paper on his desk. 'A Mr. James Holling. He lives on a new estate that's just been built.'

'You didn't mention the reason for the inquiry?'

'Now, what do you take me for? Of course I didn't. My man was working as a traveller in a garden truck. He only said that he wanted to see if the thing was a product of his firm.'

'Let's go and see Mr. Holling,' said Felix.

It didn't take them very long in Heron's car. It was a Saturday and Heron hoped that Mr. Holling was one of those people who only worked five days a week. Actually he needn't have worried, because Mr. Holling didn't work at all. He had retired.

He was considerably surprised to see them. He was stout little man with a pleasant, ruddy face, and a completely bald head, who lived in a number of very flimsy-looking villas built in the Tudor style but completely lacking in that period's solidity. Heron thought that in about five years, or even less, they would probably fall down.

The owner of Hanover Lodge, the grandiloquent name he had given his small property, was even more surprised when he heard the object of their visit.

'Yes, I bought the thing from Pigeon. Get a lot stuff from him. Why, is there anything wrong with that?'

'No, no, Mr. Holling,' said Hailsham reassuringly. 'There's nothing wrong with your transaction with Pigeon.'

'Then what do you want?' asked Mr. Holling reasonably.

Heron came to a decision. The man was obviously a respectable retired tradesman or businessman who had bought this house and its small plot of ground to potter away the rest of his days. 'If you will treat what I tell you as confidential,' he said, 'I'll explain.'

'Very well,' replied Mr. Holling a little reluctantly. 'Let me hear your explanation.'

His astonishment was almost ludicrous when he heard what Heron had to tell him. 'Good gracious!' he exclaimed. 'You surprise me! Of course, I've read about these murders, but I'd no idea . . . ' He made a feeble gesture with a podgy hand. 'It's extraordinary! Really, beyond anything I could have imagined.'

Imagination, thought Felix, was not

one of Mr. Holling's strong points.

'What do you wish me to do?' asked Mr. Holling, looking from one to the other.

'I want to examine your leaden figure,' said Heron. 'It will, I'm afraid, necessitate my cutting it open, but I shall be pleased to make ample restitution by supplying you with another.'

'That will be quite satisfactory,' agreed Mr. Holling, and there was a gleam in his eye that suggested he was only too ready to investigate the stork. 'Come into the garden.'

He unlatched the French window that gave admittance to the small garden, and ushered them to precede him. For all its smallness, the garden was a credit to Mr. Rolling's industry. It was ablaze with spring flowers that lined the trim paths and filled the symmetrical beds. At the farther end, amid a carefully constructed rockery, was a small pond. Perched on the concrete surround was a stork — one of *the* storks!

'There's the thing,' said Mr. Holling, waving his hand toward it. 'Do exactly as you wish, Mr. — er — Heron.'

Felix went over to the stork and looked at it carefully. He could find no break in the lead or anything to show that it had been tampered with in any way. It was fastened to the concrete firmly with more concrete.

'You'll need a chisel to shift that, sir,' said Mr. Holling complacently. 'I fixed it there, and I flatter myself I made a good job of it.'

'I don't really need to move it,' said Heron. He had brought a hacksaw with him which he had been carrying wrapped in paper under his arm. Taking the paper off, he gave it to Hailsham and proceeded to cut through the neck of the figure as near to the body as possible.

It didn't take long. As in the case of the other, the lead was thin and the hacksaw blade bit into it with ease. As he took the neck away, Hailsham and Holling peered over his shoulder, almost banging their heads together in their eagerness.

But the stork was empty! There was nothing whatsoever in the hollow interior.

Heron suppressed his disappointment.

'We're unlucky,' he remarked, shrugging his shoulders. 'It must be in the third and undiscovered figure.'

'It would be!' grunted Hailsham disgustedly.

'I'm sorry to have destroyed your property for nothing, Mr. Holling,' said Heron. 'But it was the only way to be sure.'

'You had my permission, sir,' said Mr. Holling with dignity. 'I'm considerably disappointed that you failed to find what you were seeking. Perhaps you would care for some refreshment?'

They went back to the house, and none of them was aware that their movements had been overlooked. But the shabbily dressed stranger whose hobby was botany had witnessed everything that had taken place in the small garden from a convenient tree nearby. As they re-entered the house he put away a pair of field-glasses, climbed down the tree, and found the bicycle which had brought him there.

Mounting this, he rode rapidly away to report to the man who had engaged him to keep a watch on Felix Heron.

$\star \quad \star \quad \star$

Mr. Holling produced a bottle of Johnnie Walker and dispensed his hospitality with a prodigal hand. Quite evidently their visit was a red-letter day in his uneventful life. He was very loath to let them go, and even invited them to lunch. He was, he told them, a widower; but he was looked after by an elderly housekeeper. He also had a son in Australia who was an engineer. They found great difficulty in getting away without being rude. But eventually they succeeded, and returned to the police station.

'Well, we know that what we're after is in the remaining stork,' remarked Heron. 'All we've got to do is find it.'

'It took long enough to find Holling's,' Hailsham grunted.

'Yes,' agreed Heron. 'In a way, I'm glad that we didn't find anything in that.'

'Why?' demanded the superintendent.

'Because we should have had to alter our plans,' answered Felix. 'The main object is not the money, but the man. We couldn't have laid the trap. Now we can broadcast the fact that we've found two to be empty. That means that the remaining one is the right one. As soon as we know where it is, we'll disclose its whereabouts *before* we go after it. Then we wait for our murderer to arrive and get it.'

'How are you going to let him know?' Hailsham asked.

'You can be sure that he's not just sitting down doing nothing,' said Heron. 'He's waiting for news, and will certainly take steps to be kept well-informed. We'll just see that he is.'

'How can you if you don't know who he is?'

'I think it can be managed,' Heron said with a smile. 'However, we've got to find the thing ourselves first. If you get any news, let me know at once.'

'Of course,' said Hailsham.

The news came sooner than either of them expected. Felix Heron had only just got back to the Manor when the superintendent came through on the telephone.

'We're in luck,' he said. 'We've found

that thing. The news came in just after you left.'

'I'll come down again,' said Heron. 'This means the beginning of the end, Hailsham.'

'I hope you're right,' said the superintendent.

Felix hung up and came out of the library. Benson was hovering about in the hall. The butler, thought Heron, always seemed to be lurking about near the library door. It might be only a coincidence; on the other hand, there was no doubt that there was somebody in the house who was working in conjunction with the man who was looking for Bannister's hoard. Gordon Lyle and Dr. Stillwater had been given permission to leave and had gone two days ago. It didn't leave many people to choose from, and Benson seemed a likely suspect.

Felix was thoughtful as he went in search of his wife. He found her on the terrace. 'I'm off to see Hailsham,' he said.

'What, again?' she remarked. 'You've only just come back.'

'I know. We're nearing the end of this

business. I've got a little job for you, dear.'

'I'm glad to hear it,' she said. 'I'm sick of wandering about doing nothing. I'm getting bored.'

'I want you to keep an eye on Benson,' he said.

'Benson? Is he in it?' she asked.

'I don't know. But he's always hanging about the door and listening. I caught him snooping again just now. Maybe there's nothing in it except my suspicious mind, but just keep an eye on him, all the same. I'll be back as soon as I can.'

'It'll be nice to see you for a change,' she said.

On the way to his car, he met Sir Richard Alperton.

'Hello, Heron. How's everything going? You seem to be always dashing off somewhere.'

'We're nearly at the end of it,' said Felix, and he hurried away before Alperton could put any further questions. As his car turned out of the drive, the shabby stranger who was poking about in a small coppice nearby, with a botanical specimen case slung over his shoulders, saw him depart. A second later he was following the car on his bicycle which had been concealed in the undergrowth.

Hailsham was jubilant. One of his men had telephoned to say that he had found the third leaden figure. 'It was given to two elderly women who live in a bungalow at Rillsham,' he announced. 'They're two sisters, name of Driscoll. They had a nephew staying with 'em, and he gave them the thing as a present before he left.'

'Probably a better present than he imagines,' said Felix dryly. 'This is fine!'

'Do you want to go over and see these women now?' asked Hailsham.

To his surprise, Heron shook his head. 'No. There's no doubt that this is the stork we're looking for?'

'This must be the one, since Pigeon didn't have any others, and it was bought from him. Why don't you want to see it?'

'There's no need. It must contain the stuff.'

'Isn't it just as well to make sure?'

'We will,' said Heron. 'Now listen . . . ' He spoke rapidly, outlining his plan. It had been ready at the back of his mind while he had been waiting for this last piece of information.

Hailsham's shrewd eyes were fixed on him. 'It's all right,' he said at last, 'so long as nothing goes wrong.'

'I don't see how it can. Tell your men to keep these two women under close observation. They're not to allow anyone to call, unless they're certain that the person or persons are well-known and above suspicion. We'll take over as soon as it's dark, and before the night is over our case should be over too.'

'Can't you give me a hint who this fellow is we're expecting?'

'I could, but I'm not going to,' said Felix. 'I'll tell you this — you'd better bring a gun. This chap will be desperate.'

'There's no certainty that he'll come tonight, is there?'

'No. If he doesn't we'll just have to continue our precautions until he does. He'll come as soon as he can, I'm sure. It depends if the news of the whereabouts of the stork gets to him in time for tonight.'

Would the night see the end of this business? It was essential that the man he suspected should be taken in the act of taking the money from the leaden figure. There was next to no case unless that could be achieved. Would he fall for the trap? Or would he be afraid that it *was* a trap? Only time would prove that.

And the whole thing depended on the accomplice in Grandchester Manor. Only through him, whoever he was, could the information be relayed to the principal. If the accomplice failed, then the baited trap would remain un-sprung. But he didn't think the accomplice would fail. And he was fairly certain that the accomplice was Benson. Someone had helped with the abduction of Kathleen Warrender; some-one had cut the telephone wires, and Benson, the comparative newcomer, was the most likely.

When Heron came in he found the butler, as usual, hanging about the hall. Felix asked where Sir Richard was.

'In the library, sir,' answered Benson.

Alperton was reading the paper. He put it down as Heron entered. 'Hello,' the former greeted. 'What's your news, if any?'

'Good,' answered Heron. 'I'll be able to tell you more when I come back.'

Sir Richard stared. 'You're the most restless fellow I've ever known,' he declared. 'You've been in and out all day.'

'Sorry, I'm afraid it can't be helped,' said Heron. 'Look, I missed lunch; do you think I could have a meal before I go?'

'Of course. What time are you leaving?'

'Six o'clock. Thelma will be coming with me and so will Harry.'

'Where are you going?' asked Alperton, and then: 'I'm sorry. I'd no right.'

'I'm going to London,' said Heron. 'I shall be be back tomorrow morning.'

Sir Richard got up. 'I suppose it's no good asking any questions, though I'm infernally curious.' He rang the bell.

'I'll be in a position to answer all your questions when I come back,' said Felix.

'Do you want a meal for your wife and secretary as well?'

'If possible, yes,' said Heron as Benson came in.

'Oh, Benson,' said his master. 'Mr.

Heron and his wife will be leaving for London at six. Will you see that a meal is prepared for them?' He turned to Heron. 'What time would you like it?'

'In half an hour, if you can,' said Felix.

A faint look of surprise showed for an instant in the butler's face. 'I'm afraid it will have to be a cold meal, sir,' he said.

'I don't mind that,' said Felix. 'Lay a place for my secretary as well.'

'Certainly, sir.' Benson withdrew.

'I'll go and change,' said Heron. 'Do you know where Thelma is?'

'I haven't seen her since lunch,' answered Alperton. Probably she's in the drawing room.'

'Don't worry, I'll find her,' said Felix, and he almost ran into her as he came out of the library. 'Listen, dear,' he said loudly, 'go and change, will you? We're going to London at six.'

She looked her astonishment. And then she saw his deliberate wink.

'Will you find Harry? I want him to come with us. There'll be a meal ready very shortly.'

'Harry's in the billiards room,' she said.

'I'll go and tell him.'

She hurried away, and Heron went up the stairs. Benson served their meal in the dining room.

As Benson left to get some orangeade for Harry — who never touched strong drink — Thelma, who had been put wise by her husband while they dressed, whispered, 'I hope it works!'

The meal was delicious, and as soon as they had finished they said goodbye to Sir Richard and left, rather ostentatiously, in Heron's car.

Twenty minutes after they had gone, Superintendent Hailsham arrived in a great flurry of excitement.

'I'm afraid, sir,' said Benson, who had opened the door in answer to Hailsham's violent ringing of the bell, 'that you can't see Mr. Heron. He left for London a short while ago.'

Hailsham was both annoyed and voluble. 'It's a great nuisance,' he said. 'An important discovery has just been made. Could I see Sir Richard?'

'I'll inquire, sir,' said, the butler. He only partially succeeded in keeping the curiosity out of his face as he went to the library.

'Superintendent Hailsham?' said Alperton, 'Yes, I'll see him. Send him in.'

Benson went back and ushered Hailsham into the library.

'I'm sorry to trouble you, sir,' said Hailsham. 'I was hoping to see Mr. Heron. Can I use your telephone? It's rather important.'

'Certainly,' answered Sir Richard.

Outside the closed door, Benson listened eagerly. There was no need to strain his ears. Hailsham's booming voice carried clearly. And he learned all that he wanted to know. He knew the whereabouts of the third stork, and something that was equally important. Hailsham distinctly said that he was going to do nothing until Heron returned in the morning.

Benson's small eyes glittered. He must get in touch with his partner as soon as possible, although they had the whole night before them.

# 14

Darkness had fallen: an intense darkness without a ray of moonlight or light of star, for the sky was cloudy. Benson made his way quickly down the drive. He had made an appointment over the telephone while the household was at dinner. He reached the gates and turned into the private road, and as he walked rapidly along, a figure that had been lurking in the shrubbery near the entrance to the avenue moved silently in his wake.

Unconscious of the follower, the butler went swiftly on until he came to the place where he had previously been picked up by the man in the car. This time the other was not so punctual. Mr. Leftwich, alias Benson, had smoked one cigarette and was halfway through a second before the dim lights appeared, came nearer, and the car stopped beside him.

'You're late,' grumbled the butler.

'Had a puncture,' answered the man at

the wheel. 'You've found out where that stork is?'

'Yes,' Benson said, with his head stuck through the window and speaking in a whisper. 'It's at a bungalow at Rillsham, belonging to two old ladies, sisters named Driscoll. That fool Hailsham telephoned old Wickthorne and told him. You could hear his bellow all over the house.'

'Where's Heron?'

'He and his wife, and that queer-looking secretary of his, have gone chasing up to London. Heron doesn't know yet that the thing has been found. Hailsham missed him by about twenty minutes. Heron's not coming back until tomorrow morning. You've got a clear run. All we've got to do is locate this place, pick up the stuff, and fade out of the picture.'

The other was doubtful. 'It sounds too easy. You're sure it isn't a trap?'

'How could it be? They don't suspect me. How do you think they expect the information will leak out? I tell you Heron's gone to London, and he went before he knew anything about it.'

'Has Pollock gone after him?'

'I don't know. I haven't seen him. He wouldn't be able to keep up with the car on a long journey. He saw them open that stork at Streatley and there was nothing in it. So the loot must be in this one.'

'It won't be there long,' grunted the other.

'What time do we go after it?' asked Benson.

'No point in leaving it too late,' said the other. 'The old women should be well asleep by midnight. Let's make it half-past.'

'I'll be waiting here at three,' said Benson. 'You can bring me my lot back with you. We can then drive to London and part company.'

'What about Pollock?'

'To hell with Pollock,' retorted Mr. Leftwich. 'He's had ten quid and that's all he'll get! He daren't make any trouble. The police have had their eye on him for a long time. Three o'clock, and don't try any funny business or you'll be sorry!'

He stepped away from the car and it moved away and vanished in the distance.

Benson turned on his heel and started back the way he had come. And behind him followed the figure which had been close at hand all the time. Unaware of this third person who had witnessed the meeting with the man in the car, Mr. Leftwich, alias Benson, strode jauntily forward.

He was feeling particularly pleased with himself. Things were working out well. With his share, he would be able to go abroad and settle down in a country where he was unknown. There were many things that a man could do with capital. And there were always ways of augmenting the original amount. He had no intention of leaving the manor empty-handed when he kept that three o'clock appointment.

But these pleasant prospects were never destined to be realised. As he entered the drive a shrill whistle broke the silence, and suddenly Mr. Leftwich found himself in the centre of a ray of light from an electric torch. He gave a gasp of surprised alarm as a hand touched his shoulder.

'I've got you,' said the voice of Superintendent Hailsham. 'I advise you to come quietly.'

The butler experienced a peculiarly unpleasant sensation in the pit of his stomach. 'I don't understand — ' he began, but Hailsham cut him short.

'Oh yes, you do,' he snapped.

'Look here — ' expostulated the butler, but he got no further.

'You're under arrest as an accessory to the murders of Norman Cassell, Arthur Warrender, and James Bannister. It's my duty to warn you that anything you say may be taken down and used in evidence later.'

'You've made a mistake,' protested the now thoroughly scared Mr. Leftwich.

'If I have, I'll apologise,' retorted the superintendent. 'Meanwhile, you're coming along to the station.'

The dapper Sergeant Cripps took him gently but firmly by the arm. 'Come along,' he said, kindly. 'It's no good making a fuss, you know.'

At that moment a slim figure in slacks and a pullover appeared in the light of the torch. 'So you've got him?' said Thelma. 'Good!'

'I suppose there's no mistake?' whispered Hailsham.

'None at all,' she declared. 'He's the man who's been working with the other fellow.'

Mr. Leftwich felt his heart sink further. 'I thought you'd gone to London,' he grunted.

'I expect you did. That was the idea. By the way,' she added, turning to Hailsham, 'there's a man over there in the shrubbery. His name is Pollock. He's a shady inquiry agent. He was engaged to keep an eye on us. I doubt if there's any charge against him but you may as well cart him along.'

'The more the merrier,' said Hailsham. 'How do you know he's still there, Mrs. Heron?'

'I'm afraid I had to use a little judo,' explained Thelma. 'He's not really hurt. He'll come to his senses in a few minutes.'

They collected the unconscious figure of the enthusiastic botanist.

'All we want now is the big fish,' said Hailsham.

'You'll get him tonight,' said Thelma. 'So far it's worked out as Felix planned. I'm sure the rest of it will too.'

Felix Heron was waiting for them at the police station, and he eyed the sullen-faced Benson with satisfaction.

'So it was you,' he remarked. 'I thought it must be.'

'Pulled a fast one, didn't you?' snapped the butler. 'Going up to London was a put-up job, eh?'

'Not a bad idea, was it?' said Felix. 'Hailsham comes along soon after I'm supposed to have gone, full of excitement with the news that the third stork has been found. He even says who had it. I guessed you'd hear and get in touch with the big fish. And that's just what you did.'

'Clever, aren't you?' snarled Mr. Leftwich.

'Reasonably,' admitted Felix. 'Now, suppose you spill the beans?'

But Mr. Leftwich refused to spill anything. It had occurred to him that there was a possibility that his partner might make a getaway. In which case there was no evidence to connect him with the matter. Therefore he maintained a stubborn silence when he was charged, and demanded that they should get in touch with his solicitor.

Mr. Pollock, vigorously protesting, was detained pending further inquiries. He produced his credentials as a private inquiry agent — it was the business cards he carried with his name and address that had enabled Thelma to identify him — and swore that had been engaged by Benson to trail Heron.

'I think you'll find he's speaking the truth,' commented Heron. 'He's nothing! Nor is Benson. The real genius behind this business is the man who will come to that bungalow tonight. Come along! It's time we got started. We can't afford to be late for the appointment!'

★   ★   ★

The bungalow was situated on the left bank of the river Thames. The soft lapping of the water as it eddied sluggishly round the piles supporting the landing-stage at the bottom of the lawn was the only sound that broke the stillness of the night. The low house, with its white veranda and background trees, was scarcely visible, its position only marked by a paler patch in the general darkness. Somewhere among the trees an owl hooted, and was answered from further afield. But that was the only sound of life. The shaven lawn sloped gently down to the river frontage, a deserted oblong of velvety turf bounded by a shrubbery of rhododendrons that were sticky with bursting buds.

There was no light in any of the windows, and the figure of the stork, perched on the edge of an ornamental pond in the middle of the lawn, might have been the brooding spirit of the place. The river moved slowly, a dark ribbon twisting irregularly between its banks, into which the leafless willows drooped pathetically. A clock in the distance struck one.

Almost at the same moment a faint sound came from the quiet river. It was the creak of rowlocks and the rhythmic dip of oars. On the black water appeared a blacker shadow. It moved at an angle from the Oxfordshire shore. Steadily it came nearer, passed mid-stream, and moved in towards the landing-stage at the end of the lawn.

The single occupant of the boat shipped his oars while he was still a few feet from the landing-stage and allowed the dinghy to drift in under its own way. The prow bumped gently against the woodwork and the man stepped deftly ashore holding the painter. Tying it to a ring, he stood listening. Only the faint rippling of the water reached his ears. He looked cautiously about, but he could see very little in the intense darkness.

After a little while he began to move up the slope of the lawn. He was almost level with the small pond before he saw what he had come for.

He drew in his breath sharply as he switched on the light of a torch. The light was dim because of the tissue paper stuck over the lens. But it was sufficient: it showed up the leaden stork perched on the stone rim — the stork that contained, that *must* contain, a fortune!

From under his overcoat he produced a hacksaw. Putting it down on the dew-soaked grass, he caught the leaden figure and tried to wrench it from its setting. The legs bent as he exerted his strength, and he twisted them this way and that until the soft lead broke.

A little breathless, he laid the thing down and picked up the hacksaw.

And the silent garden came suddenly alive! Out of the rhododendrons rushed the figures of men.

The man, muffled in overcoat and scarf, uttered an oath and pulled an automatic from his pocket. 'Keep back!' he snarled. 'Keep back!'

Hailsham hesitated. 'Don't be a fool!' cried the superintendent. 'You can't get away.'

'Drop that gun!' cut in the voice of Felix Heron, and it came from behind the other! He turned with a snarl. Heron was standing on the landing-stage between him and the boat. He held an automatic steadily pointed at the murderer.

Like a trapped rat, he stared wildly about him, but there was no way out. He was surrounded by those advancing men. He fired, pulling the trigger desperately. Heron felt the wind of a bullet as it whined past his head.

Hailsham, heedless of the gun, sprang forward and flung himself on the man, grasping his pistol-wrist. At almost point-blank range the other fired and the bullet went through the superintendent's coat sleeve, grazing his arm. They both stumbled and fell, struggling violently. Hailsham still retained his hold on the other's wrist, forcing the automatic away as the man tried to bring it round to fire again. A bullet sang over his head, and then Heron and two of the policemen went to the superintendent's assistance, and the fight was over. There was a jangle of metal, a click, and the man was helpless, his wrists secured by official handcuffs.

'Take that gun from him,' said Heron as Hailsham got breathlessly to his feet. 'The prosecution will find it valuable evidence. It killed Arthur Warrender.'

'Who is this beauty?' panted Hailsham, glaring down at the prisoner.

'Let me introduce you,' said Felix Heron. 'Meet Mr. Francis Bannister!'

'Francis Bannister?' echoed the superintendent. 'But he was killed in that motor smash.'

'Oh no, he wasn't,' corrected Heron. 'He's very much alive. But if hanging was still the penalty for murder, as it should be, he wouldn't remain so for long!'

# 15

'It's the most amazing thing I ever heard!' declared Sir Richard Alperton in the small hours of that morning when he heard what had happened. 'I'm completely bewildered. I was sure that Bannister died in that accident.'

'So were most people,' said Felix Heron. 'So was I until reason told me that Bannister was the only person who could be at the bottom of this business.'

'Who was the man who died in the motor smash, then?' asked Bob Alperton.

'A tramp named Shipple,' answered Heron. 'At least that's who we think it was. He disappeared from his usual haunts at the same time as the smash.'

In company with Hailsham and Thelma, they were sitting in the library at the manor. Dawn was not far off. The cold chill of it was in the air and they were grateful for the Johnnie Walker which Alperton had thoughtfully

provided to warm them after their arrival back.

'Well,' said the superintendent, 'it gave me a surprise. How did you get on to it, Mr. Heron?'

'I couldn't think of any other person who would fit,' replied Felix. 'So far as I could see there was no one else who could have known of the existence of this two hundred thousand pounds. By the way, it was in uncut diamonds inside the body of the stork. They had been packed in cotton wool so that there was no rattle to suggest there was anything there.' He paused to drink some whisky. 'As I was saying, Bannister was the only person who could have known they existed. He would naturally have taken every precaution to keep the fact secret. So if Francis Bannister was alive everything became more or less clear.

'I went up to Scotland Yard to see if this at first rather incredible idea could be substantiated by the facts. Chief Superintendent Manning, with whom I've worked before, and I went through everything known about the Bannister business and the alleged car accident. The first verification of my idea came when we found that Bannister's identification depended on the clothes the body had been wearing, and the contents of the pockets. His face had been so badly injured that he was unrecognisable. We found that a man called Shipple, a kind of tramp who had been in the district at the time of the accident, was reported missing. He was, roughly, the same height and build as Bannister. I should say, in justice to Bannister, that he did not plan this man's death. He only took advantage of it.'

'I don't quite understand,' said Alperton.

'You will when you hear the whole story,' said Heron.

'I think that the most horrible thing he did was kill his own son,' said Bob.

'He didn't know it was his son,' said Felix. 'He had an appointment with his confederate, Benson, in the clearing in the wood. James Bannister was in the hut and overheard enough to accuse Bannister of the murder of Cassell and

Warrender. Francis Bannister didn't recognise his son in those ragged clothes and with the growth of beard. He thought it was a stranger, and for his own safety he killed him and left the body in the hut.'

'Benson was there, was he?' grunted Hailsham.

Felix shook his head. 'Not when the murder was done,' he said. 'He'd gone. James didn't come out of the hut until he had. Probably he thought two of them were too much to tackle.'

'Poor Jim!' said Bob. 'He was a nice chap. Do anything for anybody. It was that damned girl that ruined him.'

'Why,' said Sir Richard, 'did Bannister kill Cassell and Warrender?'

Heron finished his whisky. 'The best thing I can do,' he said, lighting a cigarette, 'is tell you his own story. When he knew that a financial smash was imminent, he converted two hundred thousand pounds into uncut diamonds. These he hid in the third stork of the group in the Tudor Garden.'

'How did he get 'em inside?' asked Bob.

'He cut a hole in the underside of the body,' said Heron. 'The lead was quite thin. When he had stuffed the diamonds inside, wadded with cotton wool, he pressed the edges of the gap together and soldered it up. You could see where it joined, but of course it wasn't visible unless you looked *under* the stork's body, and then it only looked like a fault in the casting.

'But to continue. You must remember that the Tudor Garden belonged to him at the time he did this. His intention was to collect this nest-egg after the bankruptcy and go abroad. But fate took a hand in the person of the unfortunate Shipple. Bannister was driving back here on the night after he had concealed the diamonds when Shipple hailed him and asked for a lift. Although the man was a tramp in the sense that he had no fixed abode, he wasn't ragged. Bannister told him to get in the car. He was a reckless driver, and he was worried. Taking a corner much too fast, the car skidded and crashed into a tree. Bannister was stunned, and shaken, but his companion was dead. What's more, he was terribly injured. His head had gone through the windscreen and his face was mangled horribly by the glass.

'His first idea was to go for help, and then the plan occurred to him that here was a solution to his main worry, which was facing the public examination of the bankruptcy. He was a moral coward. He knew that his affairs were not straightforward. There was every likelihood of a prosecution for fraud. Here was a way out.

'He hastily changed clothes with the dead man, leaving behind the supposed dead body of Francis Bannister in the wrecked car. It seemed a perfect scheme. Nobody knew that he had picked up Shipple, and if it *was* discovered that he had disappeared, why should anybody associate him with the man in the car? As you know, nobody did. It was taken for granted that it was Bannister who died.'

As Heron paused, Sir Richard poured out another Johnnie Walker and gave it to him. He poured in a little water, took a drink, and continued.

'His first idea after he'd changed clothes with the dead man, and arranged the scene of the accident, was to come here and collect the diamonds. But it was beginning to get light already. He had quite a good distance to cover, and it was pouring with rain, to make matters worse. By the time he reached his home — his house it was then, of course — it would be broad daylight and he would run the risk of being seen and recognised. Which would have been fatal.

'He decided to go to a hotel out of the district and stop there until the night came. He caught a train at a nearby station for London and booked in at an obscure hotel. But the walk to the railway station in that pouring rain — he had had to leave his overcoat on the body — brought on pneumonia. For weeks under an assumed name he lay in hospital, more dead than alive.

'He had been carrying a few hundred pounds on him when he was taken ill, and he hoped that this would be sufficient until he could retrieve the diamonds from the stork. While he had been ill he had jotted down the hiding place on a scrap of paper in case his illness should impair his memory. In the meanwhile his house had been sold to Sir Richard Alperton and, what was worse, the stork group was no longer in the Tudor Garden!

'It was a shattering blow. He didn't know what to do. He'd taken temporary lodgings in Oxford, and he went back to them to think and decide what to do next. It occurred to him that perhaps Warrender might know something about it. He wrote to Warrender, arranging to meet him in the early hours of the morning at Cray's Lodge. Warrender must have got the surprise of his life when he got that letter from a man he had believed dead. He decided that he wouldn't do anything about it until he'd seen Bannister and heard what he had to say. Bannister had begged him not to disclose the fact that he was alive, and to make sure that no one should overhear their interview. Although Warrender had made up his mind not to be party to any fraud, he sent the servants away in deference to the wishes of his old employer.

'Bannister turned up and explained the whole situation, but Warrender wouldn't play. He refused to help. He declared that he knew nothing about the stork group, but that if Bannister had hidden the equivalent of two hundred thousand pounds in it, it belonged to his creditors. He further advised him to make a clean breast of the whole matter to the authorities, including the truth about the car accident.'

'Bannister saw that if Warrender was going to take this attitude, all his plans would be wrecked. He had relied on the solicitor being 'reasonable'. However, he pretended that he would take his advice, and Warrender came to the drive to see him off.

'Bannister attacked him, pulling an automatic from his pocket. Warrender tried to defend himself with a knife — no doubt he had armed himself with it, knowing the type of man he was dealing with — but Bannister shot him. He dragged the body into the shrubbery, picked up the knife, and went through to

251

the Tudor Garden of his old house in the hope that he might be able to find some trace of the stork group. Perhaps it had only been moved. It was, of course, just wishful thinking, but he *had* to go and make sure. We've all experienced the same feeling.

'It was while he was searching about that Norman Cassell, who had got up, probably to go to the toilet, saw him from the window and, to his utter astonishment, recognised his old employer. He hurried down to the Tudor Garden to discover an explanation for this apparently impossible sight, half believing that he'd imagined it.

'But he quickly found that it was real. Here was Francis Bannister alive! Cassell adopted the same attitude as Warrender, and for his own safety Bannister had to kill him. He was still holding the knife in his gloved hand; that's why we found only Warrender's prints on it.

'Both these crimes had been more or less forced on him to prevent disclosure, but he soon found that he wasn't safe at all! Benson, who is a professional crook, witnessed the murder of Cassell, and at the point of a gun forced Bannister to reveal the whole story. He agreed to keep silent for part of the money, when it was found, and, rather reasonably considering, fixed the price at ten thousand pounds.

'Bannister had to agree; he couldn't help himself. It had occurred to him while he was prowling about the Tudor Garden that possibly Warrender knew more about the storks and the diamonds than he had admitted. In that case, there might be something at Cray's Lodge that would tell him what had happened to the leaden group.

'He went back, threw away the knife, broke in, put Kathleen out of action by an old trick, bound her, and searched the place. It was during his search that he accidentally dropped the torn scrap from his notebook.

'The search was futile because Warrender had known nothing about the hidden diamonds until Bannister had told him. But he was convinced that he had, and he returned for another search when he attacked the constable. It was only when Benson heard about the storks, when he was listening to anything he might pick up and reported it, that Bannister realised he had been mistaken.

'That's the story. The newspapers will make a tremendous splash of it, I've no doubt. I've no wish to appear in it at all. I shall leave it to Superintendent Hailsham to explain.'

Hailsham looked at him with an open mouth. 'You mean, sir,' he gasped at length, 'that you wish me to take all the credit?'

'Exactly,' said Felix Heron.

★ ★ ★

Francis Bannister never stood his trial. On the morning before the case opened he was found, stretched out on the floor of his cell, dead. The worry and excitement had brought on a cardiac thrombosis.

'He paid the penalty, after all,' commented Felix when he heard. 'It is justice that a man who takes a life in cold blood for the sake of gain should have his own taken in return.'

'Darling!' remarked his wife. 'How old-fashioned you are! They almost give murderers medals these days!'

## THE END

GRIM DEATH
MURDER IN MANUSCRIPT
THE GLASS ARROW
THE THIRD KEY
THE ROYAL FLUSH MURDERS
THE SQUEALER
MR. WHIPPLE EXPLAINS
THE SEVEN CLUES
THE CHAINED MAN
THE HOUSE OF THE GOAT
THE FOOTBALL POOL MURDERS
THE HAND OF FEAR
THE SORCERER'S HOUSE
THE HANGMAN
THE CON MAN
MISTER BIG
THE JOCKEY
THE SILVER HORSESHOE

We do hope that you have enjoyed reading this large print book.

Did you know that all of our titles are available for purchase?

We publish a wide range of high quality large print books including:

**Romances, Mysteries, Classics**
**General Fiction**
**Non Fiction and Westerns**

Special interest titles available in large print are:

**The Little Oxford Dictionary**
**Music Book, Song Book**
**Hymn Book, Service Book**

Also available from us courtesy of Oxford University Press:

**Young Readers' Dictionary**
**(large print edition)**
**Young Readers' Thesaurus**
**(large print edition)**

For further information or a free brochure, please contact us at:
**Ulverscroft Large Print Books Ltd.,**
**The Green, Bradgate Road, Anstey,**
**Leicester, LE7 7FU, England.**
**Tel:** (00 44) **0116 236 4325**
**Fax:** (00 44) **0116 234 0205**